GET THE MESSAGE?

Fargo stepped past Clyde. "Shed your gun belts and let them drop."

"And if we don't?" the deputy who had tried to draw demanded.

"Do as he says," Deputy Olsen barked. "I'm not taking lead because you're too dumb to know when to back down." He pried at his buckle.

"The marshal will think we're yellow," the man on the horse said.

"Damn it, Tom," Olsen said.

Tom still had his hand on the Starr. A wild gleam came into his eyes and he cried, "Like hell I'll eat crow!" He jerked at his six-gun.

Fargo shot him. He put a slug into the fool's shoulder and the deputy spun half around and toppled from the saddle and didn't move. The Starr flew from fingers gone numb and landed at Fargo's feet. Fargo picked it up and gave it to Clyde. "Anyone else?"

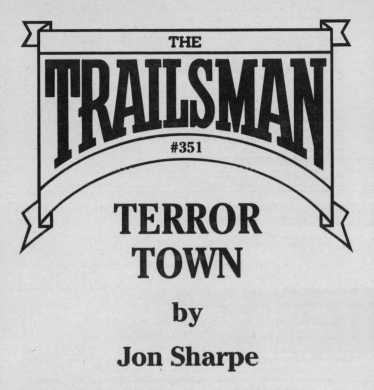

THE
TRAILSMAN
#351

TERROR
TOWN

by

Jon Sharpe

SIGNET
Published by New American Library, a division of
Penguin Group (USA) Inc., 375 Hudson Street,
New York, New York 10014, USA
Penguin Group (Canada), 90 Eglinton Avenue East, Suite 700, Toronto,
Ontario M4P 2Y3, Canada (a division of Pearson Penguin Canada Inc.)
Penguin Books Ltd., 80 Strand, London WC2R 0RL, England
Penguin Ireland, 25 St. Stephen's Green, Dublin 2,
Ireland (a division of Penguin Books Ltd.)
Penguin Group (Australia), 250 Camberwell Road, Camberwell, Victoria 3124,
Australia (a division of Pearson Australia Group Pty. Ltd.)
Penguin Books India Pvt. Ltd., 11 Community Centre, Panchsheel Park,
New Delhi - 110 017, India
Penguin Group (NZ), 67 Apollo Drive, Rosedale, North Shore 0632,
New Zealand (a division of Pearson New Zealand Ltd.)
Penguin Books (South Africa) (Pty.) Ltd., 24 Sturdee Avenue,
Rosebank, Johannesburg 2196, South Africa

Penguin Books Ltd., Registered Offices:
80 Strand, London WC2R 0RL, England

First published by Signet, an imprint of New American Library,
a division of Penguin Group (USA) Inc.

First Printing, January 2011
10 9 8 7 6 5 4 3 2 1

The first chapter of this book previously appeared in *High Country Horror*, the three
hundred fiftieth volume in this series.

The Trailsman

Beginnings . . . they bend the tree and they mark the man. Skye Fargo was born when he was eighteen. Terror was his midwife, vengeance his first cry. Killing spawned Skye Fargo, ruthless, cold-blooded murder. Out of the acrid smoke of gunpowder still hanging in the air, he rose, cried out a promise never forgotten.

The Trailsman they began to call him all across the West: searcher, scout, hunter, the man who could see where others only looked, his skills for hire but not his soul, the man who lived each day to the fullest, yet trailed each tomorrow. Skye Fargo, the Trailsman, the seeker who could take the wildness of a land and the wanting of a woman and make them his own.

The Smoky Mountains, 1861—where strangers who aren't careful wind up six feet under.

1

The two men with rifles came out of the trees as Fargo was filling his first cup of morning coffee. That they came up on him so quietly wasn't a good sign. That he was still sluggish from sleep didn't help, either. He should have heard them. He stayed calm and regarded them as if they were passersby on a street. "Gents," he said simply.

One was older than the other by a good many years. Judging by their faces and builds they were father and son. Their clothes were homespun, their boots scuffed, their hats the kind farmers favored.

The youngest planted himself and thrust his jaw out. "What are you doing here, mister?"

"Having breakfast," Fargo said. He set down the coffeepot and held the tin cup in his left hand while lowering his right hand to his side, and his holster. It was on the side away from them and they didn't notice.

"You're not from Promise?"

"Is that a settlement?" Fargo asked. So many new ones were springing up he didn't bother to keep track.

"Did the marshal send you?"

"Boy, I just told you I don't know the place," Fargo said. His right hand brushed his Colt.

"How do we know you're not lying? How do we know you're not here to arrest us?"

"Do you see a star on my shirt, lunkhead?" Fargo snapped. He was in no mood for this. Some mornings he tended to be grumpy until he'd had his coffee.

The young one colored red in the cheeks. "You shouldn't ought to talk to me like that."

"Then you should grow a brain."

That did it. The young one turned entirely red and started to jerk his rifle.

Fargo had the Colt out and cocked before the rifle moved an inch. "How dumb are you?"

The young one froze, his eyes widening in fear.

"Simmer down, Samuel," the older man said. "He ain't no lawman. If he was here to harm us, you'd be dead." The older man smiled. "I'm Wilt Flanders."

"Means nothing to me." Fargo wagged the Colt. "Have your son set down his rifle. Nice and slow."

"I will not," Samuel said. "And, Pa, how's he know you and me are related if he's not from Promise?"

"Use your head, son," Wilt said. "Do like the man wants and maybe we'll live through this."

Sulkily, Samuel bent and placed his rifle on the ground and straightened. "I don't like this."

"Then you shouldn't go around pointing guns at people." Fargo trained the Colt on the father. "Now you, old man."

"Be glad to." Wilt did as his son had and held his arms out from his sides. "There. No need for lead chucking. Suppose we just talk."

Fargo took a sip of coffee and savored the heat that spread down his gullet and into the pit of his stomach. "For nearly spoiling my breakfast I should shoot you anyway."

"Pa!" Samuel said, and glanced down at his rifle.

"He's joshing, son. Stand still and be quiet while I talk to him."

"He treats me like I'm stupid," Samuel pouted.

"Hush now, son." Wilt gestured at Fargo. "Can I come close and sit?"

"No."

"Fair enough." Wilt cleared his throat. "We have a small farm down this hill and out on the prairie a piece. We're up here after deer."

"Why would you think I was a marshal?"

"We've had some trouble with the law in Promise," Wilt said. "It's to the north, about half a day's ride."

"What sort of trouble?" Not that Fargo cared. He just wanted them to be gone so he could finish his breakfast in peace.

"My Martha refuses to wear a bonnet when she goes into town."

Fargo wasn't sure he'd heard correctly. "Martha being your wife, I take it."

"Yes, sir."

"What the hell does a bonnet have to do with anything?"

"It's against town ordinance for a female to be out in public without one on her head."

Fargo would have thought the farmer was joking if not for his earnest expression. "That is about the damnedest silliest thing I've ever heard."

Wilt smiled. "My Martha feels the same way. She says a woman should have the right to cover her head or not."

"Why would they pass such a law?"

"You go into Promise, you'll understand quick enough," Wilt said. "But I wouldn't advise it. They don't cotton to strangers much."

"Is that a fact?"

"My pa never lies, mister," Samuel bristled.

"I wasn't saying he did, peckerwood." Fargo sipped more coffee.

"The last time we were in town," Wilt went on, "the marshal told us we have to pay a dollar fine for Martha not wearing her bonnet. We had five days to pay. It's been seven and we haven't so it's likely they'll send someone to collect."

"Over our dead bodies," Samuel said.

"I won't tell you again to be quiet," Wilt said.

Fargo twirled the Colt into his holster. "You can pick up your rifles and go on with your hunt. I reckon I'll fight shy of this Promise. There are enough nuisances in my life." He gave Samuel a pointed glance.

"You'll have to swing pretty wide," Wilt said. "There's the town and the farms and a few ranches around it. Could take you a day or two out of your way."

Fargo didn't like the idea of the delay. He watched closely as the pair reclaimed their long guns. Both had the presence of mind to keep the barrels pointed down. "Off you go," he said.

They turned and went to the trees and Wilt paused to look back. "If you change your mind, be careful—you hear? I wasn't kidding about them not liking strangers. Any excuse they can come up with to give you a hard time, they will."

Father and son hiked off. Fargo kept his right hand close to his Colt until they were out of sight. He sat back, opened his saddlebags, and took out a bundle wrapped in rabbit fur.

Opening it, he helped himself to several pieces of pemmican.

He liked pemmican more than jerky. The berries mixed with the ground meat and the fat lent it a zesty taste.

The sun was half an hour high when Fargo got under way.

He held the Ovaro to a walk until he was out of the hills, and then brought it to a trot until he came to a rutted road and a sign.

He drew rein and read it out loud.

"'Promise. Twenty miles. The cleanest little town in the Smoky Mountains.'" Fargo wondered how many people were aware that there were ranges by that name both east and west of the Mississippi. He got a chuckle out of the clean comment. Frontier towns were notorious for the windblown dust that got into everything, and for droppings in their streets.

Fargo rode on. Now and then he passed farmhouses and a few cabins. In ten miles he came on a fork and another sign. It said the same thing and added in smaller letters, "'Stable service. Saloon open noon until midnight. Preachers welcome. Drummers and patent medicine men are not.'"

"Well now," Fargo said. He had a decision to make: go around or ride on through. Since he didn't much like the idea of losing a day or two, he went on. The mention of a saloon helped persuade him. It had been a week since his last drink and he would dearly love some whiskey.

A mile out Fargo came on yet another sign, the biggest and grandest yet. It mentioned that Promise had a population of one hundred and twelve souls. Harry Bascomb was mayor. Lloyd Travers was marshal.

"Good to know," Fargo said, and grinned. He'd seldom come across a town so full of itself. Gigging the stallion, he continued to the outskirts. He'd expected a quiet little hamlet with a few horses at hitch rails and not a lot of people moving about. Instead, to his consternation, the street was lined with parked farm wagons and buckboards and there had to be thirty horses tied off. Folks were everywhere, strolling about, peering in store windows and whatnot. A lot were families with kids.

A celebration of some sort, Fargo reckoned, and gigged the Ovaro. He was conscious of the stares thrown his way. But he was a stranger and that was normal.

The sole saloon was next to the general store. It was called Abe's, and the rail out front was full. Fargo reined around to the side and dismounted. He arched his back to relieve a kink and let the reins dangle. The Ovaro wouldn't go anywhere.

A stream of people flowed along the boardwalk. Fargo touched his hat to a pair of young ladies in bright dresses and bonnets, who grinned and giggled and sashayed on by. He looked around and saw that all the females wore bonnets, even the smallest girls.

Fargo pushed on the batwings. The familiar scents of liquor and cigar smoke and the clink of poker chips made him glad he had stopped. The place was packed. He shouldered to the bar and smacked the counter and a bartender with a bushy mustache and a big smile came over.

"What will it be, stranger?"

"Whiskey." Fargo fished a coin from his pocket. As the bartender produced a glass and poured, he motioned and said, "It's not the Fourth of July, is it?" He didn't make it a habit to keep up with the calendar.

The bartender chuckled. "Sure isn't. All this to-do is because of the hanging."

"The what?" Fargo said, although he'd heard perfectly well.

"Everyone is in town to see Steve Lucas strung up." The bartender glanced at a clock above the shelves behind the bar. "In about an hour. I'll be closing so I can go. It's not every day you get to see someone swing."

"No, it's not," Fargo said. The times he had, he tried to forget. It was an awful way to die.

"The mayor is going to give a speech and there are booths where you can buy juice and cakes and pie."

"Nothing like a hanging to work up an appetite," Fargo said.

About to turn away, the bartender gave him a sharp look.

"I don't know as I like your tone. The man being hung deserves it. He was caught red-handed."

"Caught doing what?"

It wasn't the bartender who answered. It was a tall, lanky man in a broad-brimmed black hat and a vest with a star on it.

"Rustling."

Fargo turned. "Marshal Travers, I take it."

The lawman nodded. He had a long, bony face and close-set eyes. "I found the cow myself in his barn."

"*One* cow?"

"One or twenty, it's all the same. Lucas stole it and he has to pay." Travers leaned on an elbow. "You here for the necktie social or some other reason?"

Fargo treated himself to a swallow of Monongahela. "For this. Then I aim to be on my way."

"Make sure you stay out of trouble. You won't like what happens if you don't."

Fargo held his temper in check and said, "You're not very friendly."

"We have a nice town here and we like to keep it that way," Marshal Travers said, and smiled. "So no, we're not very friendly at all."

2

Fargo had no intention of staying for the hanging. After the lawman walked off, he leisurely finished his drink. The bartender had mentioned it would be an hour until the hanging.

Plenty of time for him to treat himself.

Four drinks later Fargo reluctantly pushed from the bar.

The customers in the saloon had thinned some but outside there were more people than ever. He made for the general store to buy a few supplies. The store was crammed and there was a line waiting to go in. He still had time to spare so he waited and bought the flour and beans and then forced his way through the gathering throng to the side of the saloon where he had left the Ovaro.

"What the hell?"

The stallion wasn't there. Since it was rare for it to stray, Fargo figured it must have been close by. He went to the street and glanced both ways. To the right there were a lot of horses but no Ovaro. To the left there was Marshal Travers, leaning against a post.

"Looking for something?"

"My horse."

"Wouldn't happen to be a big pinto, would it?"

"A lot of people make that mistake," Fargo said. "It looks like a pinto but it's not."

"The mistake," Marshal Travers said, "was not tying it to a hitch rail. We have an ordinance against that sort of thing."

"They were all full."

The lawman shrugged. "Then you should have left it at the stable. I'm afraid you left my deputies no choice."

Only then did Fargo notice the two younger men wearing badges behind Travers. They'd had their backs to him, and now they faced around.

"What are you saying?"

"I thought I just made it plain," Marshal Travers said. "It's against the law to leave a horse unattended anywhere in Promise. First offense is a ten-dollar fine. Second offense is thirty dollars. Third offense, we take your horse and you have to go before the judge to get it back."

"You took my horse?" Fargo said, struggling to control a surge of anger.

"It's over behind the jail. We have a hitch rail there just for us to use."

"Ten dollars and you can have him back," one of the deputies said.

Fargo had splurged on the whiskey and the supplies and had about four dollars left to his name. "I don't have that much on me."

Marshal Travers straightened. "That's too bad. It means we put your cayuse up at the stable and keep it there until you can pay. And you'll be charged for the stable fees, besides."

"If I don't have the money to pay the fine, I sure as hell don't have it to pay more fees."

"How you come up with the money is your problem," Travers said.

Fargo almost hit him.

"Until you do, we keep your horse. But don't you worry. He'll be taken good care of." Marshal Travers nodded at his deputies and the three of them moved on down the street.

Cold fury washed over Fargo. He would be damned if he would stand for this. He was tempted to go after them and demand they give the Ovaro back, or else. But he had a better idea. Wheeling, he marched along the side of the general store to the rear. Farther down were a small hitch rail and five horses, one of them the Ovaro.

Fargo figured the marshal would be too busy with the hanging to check on the horses for a while. By then he would be well away from Promise.

The stallion was dozing but raised its head when Fargo opened a saddlebag to shove his supplies in. He turned toward the rail to untie the reins and heard voices inside the jail, growing louder. Quickly, he ran to a gap between the jail and the next building and squeezed in. No sooner was he safely hidden than he heard the rear door open and the voice of Marshal Travers.

"—to the stable and tell Mort I want it in a stall and not the corral. Tell him I said to strip it and put the saddle and the rest in the tack room. He's to feed it grain, not just hay."

"All that will cost extra," another man said. Probably a deputy.

"So?"

"So you heard the man. He can't pay the fine. How's he going to pay for having his horse pampered?"

"That's the whole point."

"I don't savvy."

"He can't pay, what happens to his horse?"

"We get to sell it for the fine and whatever else it will bring."

"If you knew anything about horseflesh, you'd know this

here Ovaro is a fine animal," Marshal Travers said. "I wouldn't mind owning it my own self."

"Now I get it," the deputy said. "That fella doesn't pay, you confiscate his animal and sell it for the fine money, only you buy it yourself for a pittance." The deputy paused. "Is that legal to do?"

"It is if I say it is. I'm the law. Now get the damn horse to the stable. I have a hanging to oversee."

Fargo's fury climbed. Horse stealing was itself a hangable offense. He could go to the mayor or the town council but it would be his word against the marshal's. Better to stick to his original plan. He poked his head out. The deputy was leading the Ovaro off. About to go after them, he suddenly realized the back door was still open and Marshal Travers was in the doorway, thumbs in his gun belt, watching the deputy depart. He ducked back.

It was a good minute before Fargo heard the door close. By then the deputy and the Ovaro were gone. He hastened around to the main street and spotted them at the fringe of the crowd, making their way toward the stable. Since he was the only one in Promise dressed in buckskins and he didn't want the deputy to spot him, he plunged into the thick of the gathering and worked in the same direction. There were so many people he couldn't make much progress.

Fargo was halfway when the onlookers, who had been talking and joking and eating the treats the vendors sold, fell silent.

All heads rose toward the recently constructed gallows. The press of people was so thick, he had no choice but to stop.

Up on the platform stood a short man in a suit and bowler, beaming happily. Raising his pudgy hands, he called out, "My good friends, a word before we get to it."

"What is it, Mayor?" someone hollered.

Fargo recollected the name on the sign: Harry Bascomb.

"First, I want to thank all of you for coming today. It shows a civic devotion that does my heart proud."

"Civic what?" someone near Fargo whispered to a companion.

"What's he talking about?"

"You know how Harry is. He has to speechify about everything."

Bascomb was soaking up the attention. "What we do here today is proof that Promise is as fine a community as anywhere else in this great land. We have laws, and those laws are to be abided by. When a law says a man can't steal his neighbor's cattle, then by God, he can't."

A spattering of applause rippled.

"Steve Lucas mocked the rule of law. He thought he could do as he pleased and we have proven him wrong. Lawbreakers from every walk of life must be punished, and punished swiftly. It is the mark of a civilized community."

"God, I wish he would shut up and get on with it," a man quietly remarked.

"Better hope he doesn't go on for an hour or more like he did at the church social," another said.

"Friends!" Bascomb shouted. "There's an election coming up this November. I want you to remember who stands for law and order. I want you to remember that as your mayor, I devote heart and soul to your welfare. The good of the people, that's my motto. Whatever is good for everyone must be imposed on everyone. Isn't that so?"

A smattering of agreement broke out.

"So when you see Steve Lucas, don't let his fate affect you. He's a lawbreaker and he is getting his due. Keep that thought in your head and don't let your heart be swayed."

Bascomb would have gone on but at that juncture Marshal Travers and a deputy ushered a man in shackles to the foot of the stairs.

The crowd became tense with anticipation.

Fargo didn't want to be there. But if he forced his way through, he'd draw attention, and he didn't want that, either.

He stood and watched a middle-aged man in faded homespun—Steve Lucas—sadly climb to the platform and glance in horror at the noose. Lucas stopped short and Marshal Travers pushed him so he was under the rope.

Fargo noticed that Lucas's pants had holes in them and his shoes were falling apart.

A minister dressed in black came hurrying up the steps.

He went to Lucas and they talked in low tones and the minister turned and came to the rail. "My dear friends, it is customary for the condemned to say a few words. Mr. Lucas has something he would like—"

"Is this really necessary, Reverend Peabody?" Mayor Bascomb cut in.

"It is the decent thing to do," the minister said.

"But is it necessary?" the mayor repeated with a hint of aggravation.

"When a man is about to meet his Maker," Reverend Peabody intoned, "the least we can do is grant him peace of soul."

"Fine. Get on with it then."

"But keep it short," Marshal Travers said. "We don't want to turn this into a patent medicine show."

"Of course."

Reverend Peabody put an arm around the condemned's slumped shoulders and conducted him forward.

Lucas blinked at the sun and gazed in awe at the crowd, and swallowed hard. "I just have a few words," he said, his voice rife with fear.

"Get on with it, dirt farmer!" someone yelled.

Lucas's eyes were watering. He had to try several times to speak. Finally he cleared his throat and began. "I didn't steal no cow. I may be poor but I ain't no thief and I sure ain't no rustler. I told the marshal and I told you. I don't know how Willowby's cow got in my barn. Willowby said in court that I'd made talk I wanted it for my own but I never did any such thing." Lucas gathered strength as he talked, and now he squared his shoulders. "As God is my witness, I'm innocent. All of you need to know that. I wish the jury had believed me but for some reason they didn't. So I guess this is God's will, like the reverend says, although to me it makes no kind of sense for God to want an innocent man to die." He coughed and shuffled his feet. "I reckon that's all I have to say."

"Good," Mayor Bascomb said.

Marshal Travers and the deputy moved Lucas back and the marshal slipped the noose over his head and around his neck and tightened it. The deputy slid a hood on, and right before it covered the farmer's face, Fargo saw tears glistening on both cheeks.

The reverend prayed, the marshal threw the lever, and the trapdoor dropped. But they apparently hadn't hired a professional hangman and someone had misjudged the condemned's weight. Instead of dropping straight and his neck snapping, the farmer thrashed and gurgled and kicked and took a long time dying. So long that a woman said, "God, why don't they put him out of his misery?"

Then it was over. The crowd began to disperse.

Fargo watched the body swing.

3

The stable doors were open and no one was inside. Fargo figured the stableman had gone to watch the hanging. The Ovaro was in a stall but the saddle and bridle were still on, a stroke of luck he took advantage of by leading the stallion out and hiking his boot to fork the stirrup.

"Hold on there, mister. What do you think you're doing?"

"This is my horse," Fargo said without looking to see who it was, and swung up. The saddle creaked under him and he lifted the reins to ride off.

"No, you don't." A huge man in overalls, with arms as thick as tree trunks, blocked the aisle. "Deputy Simmons said I was to keep that horse here until the marshal says different."

"You must be Mort," Fargo guessed. That was the name the marshal had used.

"What if I am?"

"Marshal Travers said for me to tell you my fine has been paid and I'm free to go."

Mort had a beetling brow that he furrowed in thought and replied, "How come the marshal didn't tell me himself?"

"He was busy with the hanging. So if you'll let me by—" Fargo was anxious to get out of there.

"I don't believe I will," Mort declared. "Climb down and we'll go see the marshal together. If he says it's all right, then you can have your animal."

"You sure are a stubborn cuss."

"I just don't want the marshal and the mayor mad at me," Mort said. "The mayor is mean when he's mad."

"How about I ride my horse to the marshal's office and you can walk with me?" Fargo proposed.

"No. It could be a trick. We get outside and you'll ride off and leave me in your dust."

Fargo sighed. Mort wasn't as dumb as he had hoped. "Whatever you think best." Dismounting, he turned and smiled and punched Mort in the gut. Normally that would double a man over. All Mort did was take a couple of steps back, grunt, and turn scarlet with anger.

"You hit me."

"Damn," Fargo said.

"You were lying, weren't you? The marshal never said you could have your horse."

"Can't blame a gent for trying," Fargo said.

"You've made me angry."

"All I want is to go in peace. Make this easy and step aside."

"I don't believe I will," Mort said, and shook his head. "No, sir. For lying to me and hitting me, I think I should stomp you."

"I have four dollars."

"What?"

"It's yours if you'll let me ride off."

"Four measly dollars to risk having the mayor close me down? Mister, you're loco." Mort balled his ham-sized fists. "Yes, sir. Pound on you fierce."

"This has been a hell of a day," Fargo said, and brought up his fists. He barely had time to set himself when Mort was on him, Mort's tree-trunk arms pumping. Fargo ducked and weaved and blocked. Each blow that connected jolted his arms to the marrow. Mort was immensely strong. Fargo sidestepped an uppercut and unleashed one of his own. Pain shot from his knuckles to his shoulder. It was like hitting an anvil. He retreated and took a straight arm to the shoulder that jarred his spine. Twisting, he whipped his fists in a flurry that brought a wince from Mort.

"That stung, mister. Maybe you should stop before you make me really mad. I'm not nice when I'm mad."

"Will you let me leave?"

"No."

"Then get set to be madder than you've ever been," Fargo said, and waded into him in earnest. He drove a right into ribs as hard as metal bars, arced his left at a cheek. Mort clipped him on the side and he shifted and slammed a straight-arm to the chin that had no more effect than the last one.

Mort's eyes narrowed in concentration and he looped his big fists in right-and-left swings. Fargo was driven back against a stall.

"Ready to give up?"

"Go to hell."

Mort glowered and rammed a fist at Fargo's face. Fargo ducked, heard a crunch, and Mort yelped and stepped back.

"I think I done busted my hand."

"Serves you right," Fargo said, and waded in again. He slammed two quick punches to the jaw and had the satisfaction of rocking Mort on his heels. Another jab to the stomach did nothing so he went at the jaw and only the jaw while trying to keep his own jaw, and the rest of him, from being broken.

Mort's greater bulk began to tell. Slowly but inexorably he forced Fargo toward a corner. Once there, Fargo would be battered into the dirt.

Fargo was desperate. He had to end it before someone else showed up. He feinted high and kicked low. His boot caught

Mort in the knee and Mort cried out and stumbled. Fargo kicked him in the other knee.

"You fight dirty!" Mort cried, and bent and clutched his right knee. "Don't do that again."

"I won't," Fargo said. He jumped straight up and arced his boot at the stableman's head.

Mort staggered but didn't go down. "Now you've done it. I'm really mad."

Mort came at Fargo in a rush, a living wall of muscle and bone and fists like sledgehammers. Fargo was forced back. He blocked a punch and nearly had his arm broken. He stepped around a stall and out of the corner of his eye spied a wooden bucket. Suddenly whirling, he grabbed the handle and swung it at Mort's head. The bucket shattered. Mort reeled, blood trickling down his scalp. He growled like a riled bear, cocked both fists, and pitched onto his chest with a thud.

Fargo was breathing heavily and ached all over. Shaking it off, he sprang to the Ovaro and was swinging up when several townspeople entered and stopped in amazement.

"What on earth?" a man in a derby exclaimed.

"Is that Mort lying there?" another said.

Fargo lashed the reins and got the hell out of there. He burst through them and out into the bright sunlight, and regretted being so rash. The street was still full of people. Some were climbing into wagons or on horses but most were standing around talking.

Fargo reined to the right, thinking to go around the stable, but a knot of gabbers was in his way. He reined to the left and had to stop. A family in a buckboard was sitting there.

The farmer's body hadn't been taken down. Up on the gallows, Marshal Travers and a deputy and Mayor Bascomb were huddled above it.

All Fargo needed was for one of the lawmen to spot him

and he would be in for it. No sooner did the thought enter his head than the deputy turned and gazed in his direction.

Fargo braced for a shout but the deputy turned back again. He gigged the Ovaro, seeking to get past the buckboard. A child of ten or so darted in front of the Ovaro and he drew rein just in time.

"Careful, there, Orville," the mother said. "You about ran into that man's horse."

The boy grinned as if it were the most amusing thing ever, and didn't move.

"Out of my way," Fargo said.

The boy went on grinning.

"Now, damn it."

"Here now," the mother said, coming and putting her hand on her pride and joy. "That's no way to talk to a child."

"I need to leave, lady, and your brat isn't helping," Fargo said.

"Well, you could at least be polite." The mother pulled on her son's arm and he reluctantly followed her.

The stallion went a dozen feet and Fargo was forced to stop again. This time two men on horses blocked the way. He couldn't go around because there were people on both sides. He twisted to find a path through them and spotted Deputy Simmons heading for the stable.

"I need to get by," Fargo said to the two men.

"Hold your britches," one replied.

The deputy was almost to the double doors.

"I need to get by now."

"Too bad," the man said, and laughed.

Fargo's patience was at an end. He reined in close and swung his fist in a backhand that sent the laugher tumbling. The other rider, stunned, gaped at his fallen friend. Fargo slipped his boot from the stirrup and kicked the riderless horse and it moved. Then he was past and only a few people were between him and the corner.

"Stop that man!"

The bellow from the gallows drew all eyes to Marshal Travers, who was leaning over the rail and pointing at Fargo.

Fargo used his spurs. He swept around the stable and onto the road to the north. Bent low in case anyone resorted to lead, he fairly flew. No shots rang out. He covered hundreds of yards and glanced back but no one was after him. That puzzled him. Travers didn't strike him as the type to let a lawbreaker get away.

Fargo didn't slow until he had put a good mile behind him.

Confident that the Ovaro could outdistance any horse alive with that much of a lead, he slowed to a walk.

Foothills rose ahead. Beyond reared mountains covered in timber. Between the hills and the mountains, by Fargo's reckoning, was the Oregon Trail. It accounted for Promise's prosperity. A lot of folks bound for Oregon Country but weary of the months of hard travel had probably decided to settle in and around Promise instead.

Fargo would be happy if he never saw the place again. He couldn't shake the image of Lucas on the gallows, and the man's last words.

Fargo rode until the sun was low on the western horizon, then reined off the road and up onto a wood-covered hill. It was as good a spot as any to make camp. He could watch his back trail and would hear if riders came in the night.

One of his ribs was bothering him. He hoped the stableman hadn't cracked it. When he climbed down, a sharp pang shot up his side. "Just what I needed." He set about gathering firewood and kindled a small fire where it couldn't be seen from the road. He had plenty of pemmican left, and with a pot of hot coffee brewing, he was as content as he could be.

The dark came alive with the howls of wolves and the cries of coyotes. Once, far off, a bear roared. Much of that country was unsettled and untamed, home to a host of beasts and several Indian tribes. Fargo wondered what the Nez Perce thought of the new settlement. They probably liked it as much as he did.

The wind rustled the trees. Occasionally Fargo heard the furtive movement of wildlife. Twice a mountain lion screamed.

Fargo was on his third cup of coffee when the Ovaro raised its head and looked toward the road and nickered. Instantly he was on his feet with the Colt out but nothing happened and after a bit he sat back down. An animal, he figured, but he stayed wary just in case.

A burning piece of limb began crackling noisily, which explained why he didn't hear the footsteps that would have warned him. He picked up the coffeepot and was about to refill his tin cup when from behind him came the ratchet of a rifle lever. He started to turn and was jabbed hard in the back.

"Sit real still or I'll shoot you."

4

The voice was younger-sounding than Fargo thought it would be, and quavering a little, as if whoever had the rifle to his back was afraid. "I'll pretend I'm a log," he said. "Go easy on that trigger."

"Joan, get his pistol," the young voice said.

To say Fargo was surprised when a girl who couldn't have been much more than sixteen came around and plucked his Colt from its holster was an understatement. He smiled at her but she was too scared to smile back. "I won't bite," he said.

The girl held the Colt in both hands and moved in front of him and pointed it. "I'm real sorry about this."

Around Fargo's other side came a boy about the same age, holding the rifle. He was sweating despite the cool of the night and his eyes were those of a rabbit that thought it might be pounced on. "We're both sorry, mister."

Fargo went on refilling his cup as if it were the most natural thing in the world to do with two people holding guns on him. "Are you outlaws?" he asked to amuse himself.

"Mercy, no!" the girl exclaimed. She had curly golden hair and wide eyes as blue as Fargo's and a cute button of a mouth. Her dress was store-bought, and expensive. "What would make you think that?"

"He's teasing us, Joan," the boy said. His hair was black,

his eyes brown. His clothes were homespun, and, telling from the patches, had seen a lot of use.

"Oh."

Fargo set down the pot. "Care for some coffee? I have plenty to spare."

"No, thanks," Joan said.

"We want your horse," the boy informed him.

"They hang horse thieves," Fargo mentioned. "Cow thieves, too, in these parts."

"We can't help it. Our horse went lame half a mile out of town." The boy shook his head in disbelief. "Of all the times for it to happen it had to be tonight."

"You're from Promise?" Fargo said to keep them talking. He took a sip. The coffee was hot but not so hot that it would blind someone.

Joan nodded. "We're running away together. We—"

"Hush, consarn it," the boy said. "We shouldn't tell him anything."

"He deserves to know why we're taking his horse," Joan said. "Be reasonable, Troy."

"If your pa talks to him, he'll know it was us."

"My father will know anyway. He's not dumb."

"No. He's snake mean," Troy said.

"I won't argue that," Joan said. "I'm just saying we ought to be nice to this man."

"Your pa hates me so much," Troy went on as if he hadn't heard her. "Him and his airs. Saying as how I'm not good enough for you. Doing all he could to keep us apart and make me and my folks miserable."

The boy's rifle had dipped and the girl had the Colt at her side. Fargo changed his grip on the tin cup so he held the bottom of the cup and not the handle.

"Not now," Joan said. "We'll talk about that later. Right now all that matters is getting to Oregon."

Troy turned to Fargo. "Which is why we need your horse. We have to get as far away as we can by morning. That's when they'll discover she's missing."

"She being me," Joan said.

"You're lovers?" Fargo said, and damned if they didn't blush.

"We're in love," Troy said. "But we've never done *that*. Not that it's any of your business."

"We're going to be married as soon as we come across a parson," Joan said.

"What's wrong with the minister in Promise?" Fargo continued to stall them.

"He's a close friend of my father's—" Joan began, and caught herself.

"Does your mother know you're doing this?"

Joan frowned. "She's been gone pretty near ten years now. Consumption. It's just been my father and me. Until I met Troy." She brightened and gave her sweetheart a tender look.

"Why are we talking to him when we should be hightailing it for the Oregon Trail?" Troy said. "If they catch us your pa will have me whipped."

"They don't do that to people anymore."

"I wouldn't put anything past your pa," Troy said. "He thinks he can do anything he wants. Look at how he lords it over the whole town."

Fargo had put together enough of the pieces to say to the girl, "Mayor Bascomb is your pa?"

"You've known who I am all along?" Joan said in surprise.

"No."

"We should tie him and gag him," Troy suggested, and glanced around. "Do you see a rope anywhere?"

"I have one," Fargo said.

Troy looked at him. "You do?"

"Yes," Fargo said, and flung the coffee in his face. He was up in a blur and wrenched the rifle from the boy's grasp.

Joan started to bring the Colt up but Fargo touched the rifle's muzzle to Troy's temple and she froze.

"Hand it over," Fargo commanded. She placed the six-shooter in his palm and he slid it into his holster and stepped back. "Now, then. Suppose the two of you have a seat." He sank down with the rifle across his lap and picked up his tin cup.

Joan looked fit to burst into tears. Troy was wiping his face with his sleeve and glowering, trying to look tough. He was about as intimidating as a five-month-old.

"Have a seat," Fargo repeated. They did, but they weren't happy about it.

"You've ruined everything," Joan said. "They'll take us back and I'll never have another chance like today."

It wasn't difficult for Fargo to figure out. "The hanging," he said. "You snuck away while your pa was busy with that."

Joan nodded. "He gave me the excuse to stay away himself. Said he didn't want me to see it. Said as how it wasn't fitting for a lady. So after he went off to town, I signaled Troy by hanging a blanket out my window and he came quick and fetched me so we could elope." She grinned at how clever they had been.

"We had it all worked out," Troy said.

"What's your last name?"

"Utley. My folks are farmers. They don't know I snuck her from her pa's country house."

"Country house?" Fargo repeated.

"That's what he calls it," Troy said. "They also have a house in town."

"Mayors must make a lot of money."

"We've always been well-to-do," Joan said. "My grandfather made a lot in business and my father inherited it. We had three houses back in the States but father sold them when we came out here."

"He gave all that up to live on the frontier?"

"He wanted his own town," Joan said. "He told me it would be easier out here than back there and he was right."

"His own town?" Fargo was making a habit of repeating what they said.

"Sure. He started Promise. Advertised in Saint Louis and elsewhere to bring people here."

Fargo thought he understood. "And he owns the general store and a dozen other businesses so he can make money hand over fist."

"Didn't you hear me? We already had enough money. He wanted his own town for the power."

"The power?" Fargo said, and inwardly swore at himself.

"He's mayor, isn't he? He runs Promise as he sees fit. In fact, he named it after a promise he made to himself that one day he would have a town all his own."

"Son of a bitch," Fargo said.

"Don't swear in front of Joan," Troy said. "She's a lady and you'll treat her as such."

Joan put her hand on Troy's. "Isn't he sweet?"

"There's one thing I still don't savvy," Fargo said. "Your father has all that, and you're running away?"

"You don't listen very well at all, do you?" Joan rejoined. "Didn't Troy say that my father doesn't think he is good enough for me? I'm not supposed to have anything to do with him." Joan fidgeted with resentment. "I'll show him. We're going to be man and wife and my father can go to Hades."

"Joan," Troy said.

"Well, he can."

"I take it you don't care for your pa all that much?" Fargo remarked.

"I hate him," Joan said. "I hate him more than anyone has ever hated anyone or anything in the entire history of the world."

"That's a lot of hate," Fargo said.

"You never had to put up with what I did. You never had someone try to control everything that you do from the time you get up in the morning until you go to bed at night."

"No," Fargo admitted. "I haven't."

"Can I have my rifle back?" Troy asked.

"No."

"Why not? Now that you know our story, you should feel sorry for us. Let us be on our way. And I'll tell you what— you can keep your horse."

"Awful kind of you," Fargo said.

"You're poking fun again, aren't you?"

Before Fargo could answer, the night was broken by the drum of hooves. Half a dozen horses or more, Fargo estimated, riding fast from the direction of Promise.

"It must be the marshal," Troy bleated. "He's got a posse out after us."

Fargo elected not to mention that the posse might have been after him. "We're safe enough here. They can't see the fire from the road."

"Yes, they can," Troy said. "How do you think we found you? There must be a gap in the trees that you didn't notice."

Fargo grabbed the coffeepot and upended it over the flames. Fortunately the fire was small and it didn't take a lot to put it out. The charred wood hissed and sputtered and a thick coil of smoke rose into the air.

"God, if they find us," Joan said to Troy.

"I won't let them take us back," the boy vowed.

Fargo was listening for sign the night riders had left the road. The pounding became thunder, and then the horses were past the hill and trotting on to the north.

"We hoodwinked them!" Troy gloated.

"They'll go as far as the Oregon Trail and if they don't find fresh sign, they'll turn back," Joan predicted. "We're not safe yet."

Fargo agreed. "Is there anywhere I can take you where you can get another horse? Back home, maybe?"

"We can't go to the country house," Joan said. "Father is bound to have men watching for me." She bit her lower lip. "We can't go into Promise, either. Too many prying eyes."

"I have an idea," Troy said. "How about we go to Miss Brubaker?"

"Who?" Fargo asked.

"She has a place halfway between here and town, and she's my friend," Joan said. "We can trust her. She's the schoolmarm. She's also about the prettiest lady you'll ever see."

"Let's pay her a visit," Fargo said.

5

The house was well back from the road. In front was a maple tree that overspread a rose garden. A buggy sat in an open-ended shed, a horse dozed in a small corral. All the windows were dark.

Fargo drew rein. He'd offered to let Joan ride double with him but she had politely refused. Troy's jealous glance might have had something to do with it.

"It's terribly late," Joan whispered. "Maybe we should wait until morning."

"How far will we get in broad daylight?" Troy argued.

Fargo wondered if they had any notion what they were letting themselves in for. It was hundreds of miles to Oregon over some of the most rugged country on the continent. There were hostiles and wild beasts and outlaws to take into account.

They'd need more luck than ten Irish to make it in one piece.

"I'll go knock," Joan said. "Miss Brubaker knows me really well."

She walked up onto the porch and rapped loudly. Presently an upstairs window glowed. It slid open and an oval face framed by shoulder-length curly hair poked out.

"Who's there?"

"It's me, Miss Brubaker," Joan called up. "Joan Bascomb."

"What on earth are you doing here at this time of night? And who's that with you out at the gate?"

"Troy Utley and a friend. We need your help. Please let us in."

Fargo was impressed that the schoolmarm didn't badger them with questions. The window slid shut and the light left the room and reappeared downstairs. The door opened and out stepped a tall woman bundled in a pink robe belted at the waist. She had a lamp in her left hand.

"Come in, young lady. Tell your friends they can come in, too."

"You go ahead," Fargo said to Troy. He had the Ovaro to consider; it could have been seen from the road if he left it there. Skirting the house, he rode to the rear and tied the reins to a lilac bush. As he walked back around he retied his bandanna and slapped dust from his buckskins. He was reaching for the door when it opened.

"Their friend, I presume."

Fargo was thunderstruck. He'd taken it for granted that Joan exaggerated when she called the schoolmarm one of the prettiest women he'd ever meet. Joan was right. The schoolmarm had the face of an angel and a body an hourglass would envy. Lustrous hair, full lips, and bright, lively eyes were frosting on the luscious cake.

"Cat got your tongue?"

"Aren't schoolmarms supposed to be as plain as dishwater?" Fargo said.

Miss Brubaker laughed. "I've never heard it expressed exactly like that, but yes, I do believe they are. I go against the grain, I'm afraid."

"If you ever need polishing, let me know."

She laughed again in genuine delight. "Oh my. I can see I'll have to keep my eye on you."

"It's only fair," Fargo said. "I'll be keeping both of mine on you."

"If I let you in, do you promise to behave?"

"If I don't promise, you won't?"

"I have my reputation to think of. As it is, I'm taking a terrible risk."

Fargo believed her. Schoolteachers were held to a higher standard than most folks. They had to be above reproach in all they did or they could lose their jobs. "I promise," he gave in.

"You're a gentleman."

"Like hell. I just don't want to get you into trouble." Fargo doffed his hat and followed her down a narrow hall to the parlor. Joan and Troy were on a settee, holding hands and trying not to look worried.

"Now, then," the schoolmarm said as she sat in a chair and crossed her long legs. "Let's hear why you woke me in the middle of the night."

While Joan explained, Fargo admired their hostess. Her bosom amply filled out her pink robe, and a suggestion of nice thighs added spice to her allure. He imagined her and him in a fevered embrace and felt himself twitch below his belt. Suddenly he realized she was talking to him.

". . . been listening? I asked why you're going to all this trouble for two young people you don't know."

"I saw her father today," Fargo said.

"And?"

"Anything he is against, I'm for."

"I see." Miss Brubaker was swinging her feet under the chair and back out again. "You're helping them to spite him. Might I ask what he ever did to you?"

"Weren't you at the hanging?"

"No. I think hanging is barbaric. In this instance, doubly

31

so. It's a miscarriage of justice that Harry Bascomb sentenced poor Mr. Lucas to die for stealing one cow."

Fargo absorbed what she had said. "Mayor Bascomb is also the judge?"

"He wears a number of hats: mayor, judge, assessor, head of the temperance league."

"That's my father," Joan said. "He always has to control everything."

"Let's forget him and talk about you," the schoolmarm said. "Is running off really wise?"

"It's the only way we can be together," Joan said.

"Her pa won't let me near their place," Troy brought up.

"As is his right as her parent and legal guardian," Miss Brubaker said. "He's not breaking the law. The two of you are."

"I'm old enough to marry if I want," Joan said.

"Not legally. You're only sixteen."

"Girls marry at my age all the time," Joan persisted. "And once Troy and I are man and wife there's nothing my father can do."

"I wouldn't put anything past him," Troy said, "which is why we're starting a new life in Oregon, where he can't touch us."

"How romantic," the schoolmarm said. "But I urge you to rethink this."

"I've made up my mind," Joan said.

"Me too," Troy said.

No one asked Fargo's opinion, which was just as well, for just then heavy hooves drummed out in front of the house.

"Sounds like I'm about to have more visitors," Miss Brubaker said.

Joan pushed off the settee. "You have to hide us, Susan. Otherwise my father will have Troy arrested and punish me in the worst way he can think of."

To Fargo it was obvious the teacher was uncomfortable with the goings-on. He half expected her to turn the pair in. Instead, she stood and motioned for them to follow her out into the hallway and over to the bottom of the stairs.

"Go up and hide in the spare bedroom. If it's who we think it is, I'll send them away."

"What if they demand to search the house?" Joan asked.

"Why should they? They have no reason to suspect you're here."

Fargo hoped not.

"Hurry. They'll be here any second."

Fargo wasn't one for tucking tail but he trailed Joan and Troy upstairs. Joan knew right where to go. He stayed by the door and held it open so he could peer out and listen.

The riders stopped. Horses nickered and voices floated up. Someone pounded on the door. Fargo heard the rasp of the bolt being thrown.

"Marshal Travers, this is a surprise."

"I'm sorry to disturb you, Susan, it being so late and all," the lawman said, not sounding sorry at all. "But I saw your light was on."

"So you brought all those men to keep me company?"

Travers took her seriously. "No. We're out after the mayor's daughter. She's been abducted."

"Excuse me?"

"Troy Utley has spirited her away. They were seen cutting across the Baxter farm earlier. The mayor is beside himself with worry."

"How do you know she didn't go with Troy willingly?" the schoolmarm asked.

"That sweet young thing?" Travers said. "Her father says she never would, not in a million years." He paused. "You haven't happened to have seen them, have you?"

"Honestly, Lloyd, at this hour?"

Fargo found it interesting they called one another by their first names.

"Well, you have a light on—"

"I couldn't sleep and got up to heat some milk."

"That should help," Travers said. "Again, I apologize for bothering you."

"They're probably halfway to the Oregon Trail by now," Miss Brubaker said.

"No, they're not. Utley's horse limped into Promise an hour ago. They're on foot and can't have gotten far."

"Good luck finding them."

"Thank you." Travers lowered his voice. "There's a social this Saturday at the church. I'd be honored if you'd accompany me."

"I'll think about it."

"Was a time when you'd say yes the moment I asked," Travers said.

"We're still friends, Lloyd, if that's what you're wondering."

"That's not what I meant and you know it. We were—"

Travers stopped. Someone had hollered, asking what was taking so long. "I reckon now isn't the time. But we need to have a talk."

"I'll come see you."

The front door closed. Fargo waited until the hoofbeats faded before he descended.

Susan Brubaker was leaning against the door with her arms folded. "Did you hear?"

Fargo nodded.

"What is it about men that a woman goes out with them a few times and they think they own her?"

"Not me," Fargo said. "I kiss them and leave them."

Susan grinned. "I bet you do."

Joan and Troy came down the stairs hand in hand. "I can't believe my father is telling everyone that Troy took me against my will," she said.

"What did you expect?" Troy told her.

The schoolmarm straightened. "You're safe here for the time being."

"We need to go while we have the darkness," Joan said. "Will you lend us your horse?"

"How will I get it back?"

"I'll bring it," Fargo offered on a whim.

"You would return my animal all the way from Oregon?" Susan said. "I could never ask that of you."

"We'll find another horse long before then," Troy said.

Susan thought a bit. "Very well. You're welcome to borrow him. The saddle and saddle blanket are in the shed out back."

"I'll do the saddling," Fargo said. He went down the hall to the kitchen and over to the back door. Cool air washed over him and he stepped out into the starry night. He had to go past the lilac bush to reach the shed, and as he did, a shadow detached itself from the lilacs and leaped at him with a club raised high.

6

Fargo dived and rolled into a crouch. His attacker came at him again. He saw that the club was a rifle the man was holding by the barrel. Starlight glinted off a metal star on the man's shirt. The stock whisked at Fargo's head and he ducked and lost his hat. Uncoiling, he landed a solid right that sent the deputy tottering. He took a bound, drawing the Colt as he moved, and slammed it against the man's temple. The deputy toppled without a sound.

Fargo whirled, anticipating more, but there was only the one. He ran to the side of the house and looked toward the road but saw no one else. Puzzled, he came back and relieved the deputy of the rifle and a revolver. He nudged him with a boot but he'd hit the man too hard for him to revive any time soon.

Fargo holstered his Colt. Bending, he hoisted the deputy over a shoulder and went into the house.

Susan Brubaker and Joan and Troy were just entering the kitchen. All three halted in surprise.

"What do we have here?" Susan asked, showing no alarm.

Fargo deposited the unconscious form on the floor and placed the rifle and six-gun on the table. "He was waiting for me."

"Alone?"

"So it seems." Fargo stepped to the sink. He dipped a ladle into a bucket of water and upended the ladle over the deputy's face.

The man sputtered and coughed and shook his head. He sat up with a start. He might have risen higher had Fargo not pointed the Colt at him.

"Deputy Olsen, isn't it?" Susan said.

Olsen rubbed his temple and fixed his gaze on Joan and Troy. "The marshal was right to leave me to keep watch. You're hiding them just like he suspected."

"And here I thought he trusted me."

Olsen continued to rub while glaring at Fargo. "You're him, ain't you? The one who stole the horse from the stable."

"A man can't steal what's already his," Fargo said.

"That's where you're wrong, mister. Your animal was impounded. You broke the law taking him."

"Tough," Fargo said.

Joan nodded at the deputy. "What do we do with him? We can't let him run to the marshal."

"We should string him up like they did Mr. Lucas," Troy said.

"No killing," Susan said sternly. "Not in my house. Not ever, young man, if you have a shred of decency."

"We'll tie and gag him," Fargo said.

Deputy Olsen had listened in growing anger. "Like hell you will. Not unless you want another charge filed against you."

"What's one more?" Fargo gave the deputy's rifle to Troy. "Cover him."

"You can count on me," the boy said.

Only when the knots were good and tight and the gag was secure did Fargo hasten back out. He saddled the school-marm's sorrel and brought it to the lilac bush and tied it next to the Ovaro. He was about to go inside when a thought struck him. He scanned the backyard and then walked to the opposite side of the house.

The deputy's horse was there, head bowed, patiently waiting.

"What do you know?" Fargo said, and grinned. He added it to his collection.

The teacher and the love doves were arguing but stopped when Fargo came in. He announced that they had three horses ready to ride.

"See?" Joan said to Susan Brubaker. "Everything is working out. If that's not proof God is on our side, I don't know what is."

"Oh, child," Susan said.

"Don't call me that."

"We should go," Fargo advised, but no one seemed to hear him except the deputy who mumbled through his gag.

"I wish you would reconsider," Susan told the pair. "It's a big step, marriage. Not one to be taken lightly."

"We love each other," Joan said.

"Sometimes love isn't enough."

"I have listened to all I'm going to." Joan grabbed Troy's hand and pulled him toward the back door, saying to Fargo as they went by, "Are you coming or not?"

"Talk to them," Susan said. "Convince them of the error of their ways. You're old enough to know, like me, that they're making a mistake."

"I've made a few of those myself." Fargo smiled as he went out but she didn't return the gesture. The lovers were already in the saddle. Forking leather, he instructed them, "Hold to a walk until I say not to."

Toward town a dog howled.

Fargo flicked the reins. The breeze refreshed him. He'd had a long day and could have used the good night's sleep the ride would deny him.

They were almost to the front of the house when from out of the dark a voice bellowed, "Halt in the name of the law!"

It was Marshal Travers. Deputy Olsen had lied about being alone.

"Ride like hell!" Fargo shouted at Joan and Troy. He resorted to his spurs and the Ovaro exploded into motion. Men materialized in the gloom, some on foot, some on horseback. A deputy lunged and grabbed his leg, seeking to unhorse him, but the stallion was moving too fast for the man to hold on. Another deputy on horseback brought his animal broadside. Fargo reined around and galloped on.

"Stop them!" Marshal Travers bellowed. "Do you hear me? *Stop them!*"

Like hell, Fargo thought. He would cheerfully ride right over the next son of a bitch who got in his way but fate smiled on him and he blended into the night unscathed. He thought the others were behind him until a horse squealed and he glanced back, and swore.

Men had hold of Troy's mount and were pulling him from the saddle. Troy fought but he was one to their four. Joan stopped to go to his aid and was promptly surrounded.

Short of shooting the deputies or risk being caught himself, there was nothing Fargo could do. He galloped on. No one came after him. They only wanted Joan and Troy. He rode until he was out of earshot and drew rein. He had another decision to make. He didn't owe the pair anything; they owed him. They weren't kin or friends, they were acquaintances. He could ride on with a clear conscience. Then he thought of how Travers impounded the Ovaro, and of that farmer, Lucas, and the gallows.

Marshal Travers was collecting his posse. Troy, bound wrist and ankles, was thrown belly down over a horse. Joan was permitted to ride but two deputies hemmed her.

Susan Brubaker was on her porch, her arms across her chest.

"I'm sorry, Joan," she called out. "I truly am. But there's nothing I can do."

Travers touched his hat brim and the posse trotted toward Promise.

Fargo shadowed them. The position of the North Star told him it was pushing midnight when they got there. The marshal rode down main street to the jail and two deputies hauled Troy inside. Joan was escorted to a house that took up two lots and was the closest to a mansion of all the buildings in Promise. Travers personally took Joan to the front door. The mayor must have been waiting up because it opened at the first knock and there he was. From his gestures and his tones, he was giving his daughter a tongue-lashing.

Fargo had seen enough. He circled wide and was at the schoolmarm's by one. Her place was dark again. He tied the Ovaro to the same lilac bush and knocked on the back door and went on knocking at half minute intervals. She was a while getting there. She peeked out the window, saw him, and came to the door and opened it wide enough to frame her face.

"You again? I assumed you would be miles away by now."

"If I had any sense I would be."

"Why are you here?"

Fargo gave her his best smile. "I thought you might put me up for the night."

"My reputation, remember?"

"I'll leave before first light. No one will know but you and me."

"You're terribly bold."

"All I'm asking for is a bed to sleep in," Fargo said. "My

intentions are honorable." The fib tripped off his tongue as naturally as anything.

She hesitated, then sighed. "I suppose it's all right." She stepped aside and when he was in she quickly shut the door behind him. As she turned she tugged the robe up around her neck. "You can sleep on the settee."

"What's wrong with the spare bedroom?"

"It's upstairs and I prefer you downstairs," she bluntly replied.

"It's your house."

"Yes, it is." She brought blankets and a pillow to make himself comfortable, bid him good night, and climbed the stairs.

Fargo stretched out on his back with his legs over the end. He left his boots on and his gun belt around his waist.

Sleep was a feather tickling his brain. It eluded him until finally his weary body succumbed. He slept as one dead and was awakened by the aroma of brewing coffee and food being cooked. Casting the blankets off, he rose and shuffled to the kitchen.

"You didn't have to feed me, too."

Susan was busy at the stove. "It wouldn't be hospitable to send you off hungry. Have a seat."

Fargo had to hand it to her. She could cook. The eggs were done to perfection and the bacon wasn't too crisp or too raw. She smeared butter and jam on several slices of toast and brought them over. "How about you?" he asked.

"I'm not hungry."

"I never get enough," Fargo said, and ran his eyes down her body.

"You promised."

"It's up to you whether I keep it." Fargo took a bite and chewed with relish.

"I'd rather you did," Susan said.

Fargo chuckled.

"I'm not amused at you wanting to ravish me. It doesn't interest me in the least."

"Your eyes say it does." Fargo speared a slice of bacon thick with juicy fat.

Susan was taking the eggs to her pantry, and stopped. She regarded him thoughtfully. "I'll admit that you are ungodly handsome but that's all I'll admit."

"It's a start," Fargo said. He cut an egg white and forked it into his mouth and ate slowly.

"Do you do everything with as much zest as you eat a meal?" she asked.

Fargo looked her in the eyes. "Everything."

Susan blushed and went into the pantry. When she came back out she had composed herself enough to say, "I think you're trouble with a capital T. Do me a favor and don't come back. I never want to see you again."

"You're not being honest."

"Says who? I'd like to see you prove it," Susan said defensively.

"I will," Fargo said.

"Oh really? When?"

"Tonight."

7

Dawn had barely broken when Fargo drew rein at the hitch rail behind the jail. Only one horse was there. He quietly tried the back door but it wouldn't open. Drawing his Colt, he walked around to the front and in the front door.

Deputy Simmons was asleep at a desk. His boots were propped on the desktop and he was snoring loud enough to rattle the gun rack.

Fargo stood with the Colt level at his hip. "Rise and shine."

The deputy mumbled and snorted and abruptly sat up, shaking his head to clear it. His boots dropped to the floor and his eyes widened in amazement. "Are you plumb loco? Marching in here like this and pointing a pistol at me?"

"Troy Utley," Fargo said.

"What about him?"

"I'm posting his bond."

"What the hell are you talking about? The judge hasn't gotten around to setting any yet."

Fargo waggled the Colt. "This is his bond. Get up. You're letting him go."

Simmons thrust out his jaw. "Like hell I am. The marshal would have my hide." He grinned craftily. "Go ahead and shoot. It'll bring folks on the run and then where will you be?"

On the wall behind the deputy was a peg and hanging from the peg a large key ring.

"Are those the keys to the cells?" Fargo asked.

Simmons shifted in his chair to look at them. "No. Those are . . . uhhhh . . . the front and back door keys."

Fargo casually walked around the desk. "You're terrible at lying," he said, and slammed the Colt against the deputy's head.

Simmons folded in half and melted to the floor. Grabbing the ring, Fargo stepped to the door that separated the office from the cells. It wasn't locked. Only one cell was occupied. There was no light and in the dark it was hard to see who was curled on their side with their back to the bars. "Utley?"

The figure stirred and rolled over. "Who's there?" he sleepily asked.

"Rise and shine," Fargo said. "You're leaving." Four keys were on the ring. The second was the right one. He pulled on the door and the boy stepped unsteadily out. "Are you all right?"

"They beat on me a little."

Fargo stepped to the back door and slid the bolt. "We'll borrow the deputy's horse."

"I might need a boost."

Fargo had a good look at him, and swore. The boy's face was black-and-blue, one eye was swollen shut, and one ear was twice the size of the other. Dry blood flecked his chin and his lips were puffy. He was holding his right hand against his side, and limping.

"Who did this?"

"The marshal, with a little help from Joan's pa."

"Let me see that hand." Fargo took hold of the arm, and Troy flinched. The knuckles were swollen to the size of walnuts and the thumb stuck out at an angle that no thumb should. "It's broken."

"The marshal stomped on it when I wouldn't confess to taking Joan against her will."

44

"You need a sawbones."

"The doc is a good friend of the mayor's," Troy said. "We go there, he'll let the law know." He put his other hand on Fargo's arm. "Take me home. My folks will take care of me. My ma has set plenty of busted bones."

Fargo helped him onto the horse and handed up the reins. "Lead the way."

Lights were coming on. Early risers were up and about.

Troy stayed close to the backs of the buildings until he was at the south end of Promise and then reined off across the farmland.

Fargo stayed at his side. The boy was in a bad way and grimaced in constant pain.

They swung wide of every dwelling and farmhouse. Once a dog barked at them but no one came out to investigate. The sun was a couple of hours high when they climbed a low rise. Troy pointed and made for a small house with a barn nearby, saying excitedly, "That's our place."

"Slow down," Fargo cautioned. He had a hunch the boy was as busted up on the inside as he was on the outside and trying hard not to show it.

"You have to promise me something," Troy said.

"Depends on what it is."

"Don't let my pa go off half-cocked. He's liable to want to kill the marshal."

"Can't say as I blame him."

"That's not the point. My pa is no gun hand. Hell, he hardly ever hunts anymore. Promise me you won't let him get himself killed."

"I'll do what I can."

Smoke curled from a chimney. Chickens pecked at the dirt and hogs rooted in a pen. There was no sign of anyone outside.

"My ma must be fixing dinner," Troy said. "I hope she can forgive me, running off like I done."

The small barn and a few outbuildings were all the farm could boast. A handful of cows grazed or dozed in the heat.

Troy tried to climb down and nearly collapsed. Fargo helped, and steadied him when he swayed.

"You're a lot worse off than you've let on."

"I didn't want to slow us."

Fargo hooked his arm under the boy's and started toward the back door. "Lean on me if you have to."

"They're going to hang me," Troy said.

"I doubt that," Fargo said. Not when Joan would testify that the pair had run off together.

"The mayor told me. Said he was personally going to see to it that I swing just like Mr. Lucas."

"Did he, now?"

Troy nodded, and flinched. "He told me that no daughter of his was going to have white trash like me for a husband. That's what he called me. White trash."

Fargo avoided a wheelbarrow with a rake in it.

"Am I, mister?" Troy said.

"Are you what?" Fargo saw a shadow move across the kitchen window.

"White trash? The mayor says poor folks like us are a blight. What's that mean, exactly?"

"That someone should shove a six-shooter up the mayor's ass and use it for target practice."

"Is it wrong, me wanting to be with Joan? With her being so rich and all and me being so poor?"

"Why are you asking me?"

"I don't know who else. I can't tell my ma and pa what the mayor said. It would hurt their feelings."

Fargo stopped. "Do you care for her?"

"Joan? With all my heart. I'd do anything for her."

"There's your answer."

"You must be a romantic cuss like Joan says I am."

"Hell," Fargo said.

"When she told me she loved me, it was the happiest day of my life. A girl as fine as her. And she wants to spend the rest of her days as my wife. Ain't that something?"

Fargo was spared having to answer by a portly woman in an apron who opened the back door.

"Troy!" she squealed for joy, and lumbered out to enfold him into her fleshy arms. "God Almighty. What's happened to you, son? Who did this?"

"Ma," the boy said, and collapsed.

She caught him before he could fall.

"I'll take him," Fargo offered.

"No, you will not."

Fargo held the door and Mrs. Utley carried her son through a cozy kitchen and up a flight of stairs to a bedroom. She gently laid him on his back and tenderly touched his battered face. Tears welled but she held them back.

"I'll ask you, mister. Who did this to my son?"

"The mayor and the marshal."

"Over that girl?"

Fargo nodded.

"My name is Rosemary, by the way. I thank you for helping him." She gestured. "Would you mind heating up a pot of water for me? The pump is around to the side." Rosemary unbuttoned her sleeves and began to roll them up. "I have doctoring to do."

"There's something you should know," Fargo said. "They'll be coming for him."

"The law?"

"Yes, ma'am."

"Lordy, Clyde will be furious." Rosemary took a deep breath. "But we'll deal with that when it happens. In the meantime, do you mind heating that water?"

Fargo found a pot in a cupboard. The pump handle took some effort. He had to work it a dozen times before water spurted. He was setting the pot on the stove when a horse galloped up. Putting his hand on his Colt, he turned.

The man who barreled inside was the spitting image of Troy, only forty years older. His face had the weathered look of someone who spent a lot of time outdoors. He wore an old flannel shirt and britches with suspenders and beat up boots. "I thought I saw riders when I was mending my fence. Who might you be, mister, and why are you in my house?"

"You must be Clyde," Fargo said. "I brought your boy home. He's upstairs with your wife."

Without another word Clyde dashed from the kitchen. His boots thumped the stairs and there was a bellow of anguish and rage.

Fargo leaned against the table. He noticed a shotgun propped in a corner.

Not a minute later the boots thumped again and Clyde Utley stormed into the kitchen muttering furiously, grabbed the shotgun, and broke it open to load it.

"Do that to my boy! I'll show them! Who do they think they are, beating on him like that? Breaking his hand." Clyde closed his eyes and groaned. "That boy never hurt a soul."

Fargo went over and gripped the twin-barrels. "You can't do your son any good dead."

Clyde's eyes snapped open. "You! I forgot you were here." He sought to wrest the shotgun loose. "Let go. You saw what they did. Those varmints need to pay."

"You ever killed a man, Clyde?"

"No. But I can if I have to. Now let go, damn it." Clyde pulled harder.

"Can't," Fargo said.

"Why in hell not?"

"Your boy asked me to keep you here."

"Troy what—?" Clyde let go of the shotgun and stepped back and bowed his head. "God help me. What am I to do? They can't get away with this."

"They won't."

Clyde tried to square his shoulders and look tough, his eyes as wet as Rosemary's had been. "Why are you mixed in this?"

"The marshal and the mayor did something they shouldn't have."

"What?"

"They pissed me off."

Clyde studied Fargo as if seeing him for the first time.

"What can we do? The mayor has the law on his side. And Travers has several regular deputies and can call on more men, besides."

"Six or twenty-six, it's all the same," Fargo said.

"You mean because we have right on our side?"

"No." Fargo patted his Colt. "Because I have this."

8

The four riders raised a lot of dust. They swept down on the farm with the sun gleaming on their badges.

Clyde came out to meet them, unarmed. Rosemary stood in the doorway.

Deputy Olsen didn't waste time on small talk. He leaned on his saddle horn and said, "We're here for your boy, Utley. An outlaw broke him out of jail and I'd bet my poke they came straight here."

"What was my son doing behind bars?" Clyde asked.

"As if you don't know," Olsen said. "He was arrested for abducting the mayor's girl. We aim to have him so you'd be smart to hand him over."

"Why didn't Marshal Travers come with you?"

"He's staying close to the mayor for the time being so he sent us. Now hand over your boy or we'll come in and take him."

"You can't barge into a man's home because you feel like it," Clyde said. "Don't you need something called a warrant?"

"Listen to the lawyer, boys," Olsen said to the others, and they laughed or smirked. "Yes, you stupid farmer, we can. We're the law and you'll do as we damn well want."

"You're not stepping foot in my house."

"We'll see about that." Olsen nodded at another deputy

and the two of them climbed down. Olsen hitched at his gun belt and looked his most menacing. "Get out of our way or we'll go through you."

"No, you won't."

"What's to stop us, you jackass?"

Fargo stepped around the corner with his right arm at his side. "Me."

Olsen and the other deputy both froze but one of the men on horseback stabbed a hand for a Starr revolver, blurting, "It's the one who rides the pinto!"

Fargo drew. His Colt was out and cocked and level before the deputy on the horse could blink. "I wouldn't."

The man stiffened and his face turned chalky. "Don't shoot. Please."

"Hell in a basket!" the other deputy on horseback marveled. "I didn't see his hand move."

Fargo stepped past Clyde. "Shed your gun belts and let them drop."

"And if we don't?" the deputy who had tried to draw demanded.

"Do as he says," Deputy Olsen barked. "I'm not taking lead because you're too dumb to know when to back down." He pried at his buckle.

"The marshal will think we're yellow," the man on the horse said. "We're wearing the badges. This son of a bitch has to do as we say, not the other way around."

"Damn it, Tom," Olsen said.

Tom still had his hand on the Starr. A wild gleam came into his eyes and he cried, "Like hell I'll eat crow!" He jerked at his six-gun.

Fargo shot him. He put a slug into the fool's shoulder and the deputy spun half around and toppled from the saddle and didn't move. The Starr flew from fingers gone numb and landed at Fargo's feet. Fargo picked it up and gave it to Clyde. "Anyone else?"

"No, sir," Deputy Olsen said. He tossed his gun belt to the grass. "See? Meek as lambs. That's us."

"You appear to be the brains so you can give Travers a message for me," Fargo said.

"You can give it to him yourself when he comes after you," Olsen replied. "And he will, mister. Lloyd Travers was a law dog down in Texas before he took this job. He's broken more badmen than you can count."

"Like he broke Troy Utley's hand?"

Deputy Olsen didn't answer.

"I'm not a badman and I'm not a boy," Fargo said. "You tell Travers he won't have to come looking for me. I'll be coming for him."

"You ride into Promise, you're a dead man."

"Give the same message to the mayor."

"You *are* loco," Olsen said. "You can't take on a whole town. If he has to, the mayor will call out every man in Promise and Marshal Travers will deputize them."

"Half a mile," Fargo said.

"How's that again?"

"I can drop a buffalo at half a mile with a Sharps." Fargo wasn't exaggerating. But he didn't use a Sharps these days. He used a Henry, which held more shots but lacked the Sharps's range. But they didn't know that unless they'd checked his saddle scabbard.

"What are you saying?" Deputy Olsen said. "That you'll lie on the prairie somewhere and pick them off when they step into the street?"

"Something for them to think about," Fargo said.

The deputy who had been shot sat up, clutching his shoulder. "What happened? Why am I—?" He cursed. "Now I remember. That bastard shot me."

"Get on your horse, Tom," Olsen said. Wheeling, he climbed on his own. "This ain't over, mister. Not by a long shot."

"No," Fargo said. "It's not."

Rosemary came out and stood watching the deputies ride off.

"Thank you for helping us. If you hadn't been here—" She didn't finish.

"I'd have protected you," Clyde said.

"I love you dearly," Rosemary said, "but you couldn't do what he did."

"I have a lot of practice," Fargo said, and changed the subject. "How's your son?"

"Sleeping. I set his hand and put his arm in a sling. There's not much I can do for his ear. The swelling will have to go down on its own."

"Where can I find the mayor's country house?"

"You're paying him a visit? By your lonesome? Is that wise?"

"I won't know until I get there."

"He'll have men watching over it."

"The people of Promise," Fargo said. "Where will they stand?"

"Believe it or not, most folks like Harry Bascomb," Rosemary said. "So did we until our son started courting his daughter. Then one day Bascomb came over and sat us down and said we should use our influence to break them up."

"The nerve of the man," Clyde said.

"We told him our son was almost full-grown and could do as he pleased."

"How did the mayor take that?"

"Like we had kicked him in the teeth," Clyde said. "He warned us if we didn't do as he wanted, there would be hell to pay."

"Bascomb showed his true colors that day," Rosemary said. "I would never have thought he's as mean and spiteful as he is. He hides it well."

"So tell me about the country house."

It wasn't as big as the mayor's house in Promise but it was finer than any farmhouse or ranch house in the whole countryside. Situated in woods along a winding creek, it had a balcony on the second floor that overlooked a neatly maintained lawn.

Fargo noted the comings and goings from his hiding place in the trees. A deputy was on the porch, looking bored. From time to time another came out and made a circuit of the grounds and went back in. The only other person Fargo saw was a black man puttering around in the stable.

The sun was almost gone when Fargo rose. The black man was forking hay. When Fargo touched the Colt to the nape of his neck, the man imitated a board.

"Drop the pitchfork."

"Yes, sir." The man raised his arms. "If it's money you're after, Mr. Bascomb has all of his in the bank."

"How many people are in the house?"

"Two deputies the marshal sent and the missus."

"Joan Bascomb?"

"Yes, sir. They brought her out about noon. What is she to you?"

Fargo stepped back. "Turn around." When the man complied, he asked, "Where do you stand in this?"

"In what, if you don't mind my asking?"

"Joan and Troy Utley."

"Oh. That. I'm the stableman. I keep my nose out of the family's affairs."

"You've heard that Utley kidnapped her?"

"A deputy said as much, yes. Not that I believe him."

"Why not?"

"Miss Joan is nice. She talks to me, brings me cookies. Her pa can't be bothered. To him I'm just another darkie. But he pays well so I swallow my pride." The man paused. "I've seen them together, Miss Joan and the boy. He sneaks over a lot after the sun goes down and they meet out back and do what young folks always do when they're like they are."

"I'm taking her to him. You won't try to stop me?"

"No, sir. I'll just go to my room at the back of the stable and stay there until they send for me and if they ask I'll say I never saw you nor talked to you nor had anything to do with whatever you did."

"I'll take you at your word."

"That's more than most would do."

The deputy on the porch was in a rocker with his boots on the rail. He was admiring the sunset. He wouldn't have heard Fargo if a board hadn't creaked. When the deputy turned, Fargo sprang. He slashed the Colt at the deputy's head but the man shifted and he missed. Before he could swing again the deputy heaved out of the chair and threw himself at Fargo's legs. Fargo was bowled over and came down on the same side as his hurt rib. The pain was excruciating. He twisted and the deputy was on him. A hand clamped onto his wrist and a knee rammed into his chest. Fargo pushed but the deputy clung on. With a wrench Fargo tore free and made it to his knee.

The front door opened and out rushed the other deputy, a Smith & Wesson in his hand. He snapped a shot that tore into the boards inches from Fargo's leg. Fargo snapped a shot of his own and the deputy went down.

"No!" the first one roared, and was on Fargo in a flurry of fists. Fargo's jaw rocked to a punch. His cheek was hit. He slammed the Colt across the deputy's throat and the man lurched and gurgled. Fargo smashed a blow to the head and the man collapsed.

Holding his arm to his side, Fargo rose and threw the Smith and Wesson and the other hogleg into the grass.

The house was quiet. The lamps hadn't been lit yet and the rooms were in shadow. He went from one to the other and didn't find Joan. A spiral staircase brought him to the second floor. The four bedrooms were empty. He was beginning to think the black man must be wrong and she wasn't there when he came to a glass door that opened onto the balcony.

She was in a chair that faced to the west, and the sunset. Her head hung low and her hair was half over her face.

"Joan?" Fargo holstered the Colt.

"Who?" she said. Her eyes were dilated and she moved terribly slow.

"What did your pa do to you?"

"The doctor," she mumbled. "Gave me something so I couldn't run away again."

"Would you like to go to Troy?"

"Yes. Oh, yes. I've been so worried—" She drew her head back and said, "Look out."

Fargo whirled.

The black man was coming toward him—and holding the pitchfork.

9

"What do you think you're doing?" Fargo said.

"I can't let you. I'm sorry but I can't."

The man leaped and speared the tines at Fargo's neck. Fargo skipped back, swooping his hand to his Colt. His foot caught on Joan's chair and he lost his balance and fell against the rail. His wrist slammed hard and the Colt went sailing out and over and landed in the grass below.

"Cyrus, no," Joan cried.

"I'm sorry," the black man said again, and lanced the pitchfork at Fargo's belly.

Fargo tried to sidestep and felt searing pain. A tine had pierced his buckskin shirt and drawn blood. He lunged for the handle but Cyrus was too quick and leaped clear. Fargo retreated along the rail, his eyes glued to the tines. "Why?"

Cyrus moved the pitchfork in small circles, his eyes intent. "I don't stop you, maybe Mr. Bascomb will get mad. Maybe he'll fire me." Cyrus stopped and gazed fondly toward the stable. "This is the best job I ever had, mister. I ain't about to lose it on account of you."

Joan was struggling to stand. "Listen to me, Cyrus. You mustn't do this. He's here to help me."

"I'm sorry, missy. But your pappy says you've been a bad girl and this is for your own good."

"Cyrus, please."

Cyrus looked at Fargo. "Were I you, I'd jump. You might break a leg but I give you my word I'll let you go."

"Like you gave me your word at the stable?"

"We do what we have to," Cyrus said, and came at Fargo with the pitchfork flashing. Fargo jerked back and the tines missed his eyes by a whisker. Again and again Cyrus stabbed. Again and again Fargo dodged and slipped aside. He realized that Cyrus was forcing him toward the wall and tried to bound into the clear. The tines swept at his neck and he had to retreat farther.

"Cyrus!" Joan cried. She was almost to her feet but sank down.

Cyrus attacked, and Fargo bounded out of reach and pretended to stumble. Dropping to his knee, he grabbed at his ankle as if he was in pain.

Cyrus raised the pitchfork. "You should have gone over the rail when I gave you the chance."

"Cyrus, no!"

By then Fargo has his hand in his boot and his fingers around the hilt of the Arkansas toothpick. Cyrus thrust at his chest. Swiveling aside, Fargo sank the blade into Cyrus's wrist. Cyrus hollered and jerked back and the toothpick opened him to his elbow. Dropping the pitchfork, Cyrus pressed his other hand over the spurting gash.

"Are you done now?" Fargo said.

Cyrus turned and fled.

"Let him go," Joan said. She was almost to her feet. "He's really a nice man."

"When he isn't trying to kill you," Fargo said.

"Get me out of here."

Fargo swept Joan into his arms and carried her from the balcony and along the hall to the spiral stairs. Her head kept bobbing and her eyes moved back and forth in their sockets.

"I'm so woozy I can't hardly think."

"Rosemary will take care of you," Fargo said. He could have used some mending himself. His cracked rib was on fire and where the tine had stabbed him hurt like hell.

"You've met Troy's mother? Isn't she the most kindly woman in the world."

The front door was open. Through it Fargo saw Cyrus a few yards from the porch, awkwardly turning the Smith & Wesson in his hand. "Son of a bitch."

"What's wrong?"

"Your wonderful Cyrus is thinking of shooting me." Fargo ducked into a sitting room and placed her on a sofa. "Stay put and keep quiet."

"But I—"

"Not a damn word." Fargo moved to the doorway.

Cyrus stalked inside and moved toward the stairs. His right arm dripped blood. In his other was the Smith & Wesson, cocked.

Fargo waited until Cyrus was around the first spiral. He sprinted out the front door and was across the porch and in the grass, searching for his Colt. He gauged about where it should be but it wasn't there so he roved in a circle and back again. Another step, and his boot came down on something hard.

Above him a revolver cracked and lead bit into the earth.

Fargo lifted his foot. Under it was the Colt. He scooped the revolver up even has he flung himself aside. Above him there was another shot. He thrust the Colt out and up and centered it on the dark shape leaning over the top rail. He fired once, twice, three times.

Cyrus reared onto his toes. He clawed at the air and his mouth worked. In slow motion he keeled forward and gravity took over. He slammed into the ground with a pulpy thunk and blood spurted from his nose and ears.

Fargo stood and stared into the lifeless eyes. "Bascomb wasn't worth it."

"Fargo?" Joan hadn't listened. She was in the doorway, gripping both jambs, her legs shaking like tree limbs in a storm.

Fargo reached her before she fell and she passed out in his arms. He tried to bring her around but she wouldn't respond. To get her on the Ovaro he first had to sling her over the saddle like a sack of flour, then climb on and sit her up in front of him with his hand around her waist.

The ride to the Utley farm seemed longer than it was. The moon was well up when he tiredly drew rein.

Rosemary and Clyde must have been listening for him. They came out before he could climb down and gave him a hand with Joan.

"Awful, just awful," was Rosemary's assessment of the state of affairs. "That they would do this to a young girl."

"Her pa has no shame," Clyde said.

They tucked Joan into bed. In the next room Troy was sound asleep.

"I saved some supper for you, just in case," Rosemary said. "Would you like to eat?"

Fargo was famished. The meal was simple fare, stew and bread, but delicious. The vegetables came from their garden and she had baked the bread that morning. He smeared each slice thick with butter and dipped it in the broth. To wash it down he had four cups of coffee.

Rosemary sat across from him, saying little until he pushed back his bowl and patted his stomach.

"I'm obliged, ma'am."

"And I'm worried, Mr. Fargo. What do you think will

60

happen? Will the marshal come and arrest our son? And arrest us too, maybe, for not letting those deputies take him?"

"I was the one sent them packing," Fargo said. "It's me they'll be after."

"We both know that people like Mayor Bascomb stop at nothing to get their way. He's a prideful man with no regard for others."

"He's a son of a bitch," Fargo said.

"It's a shame more don't realize it. Although there have been whispers about poor Mr. Lucas. I heard some at the general store."

"Care to share?" Fargo said when she didn't go on.

"Willowby, the man who accused Mr. Lucas of stealing his cow, has one of the biggest farms in the area. But he's always had a problem with water. His wells have to be dug deep and don't produce a lot, and his creek isn't year-round."

Fargo saw where it was leading. "Lucas's place?"

"Good wells, and a pond that never dries up. And it borders Willowby's."

"The whispers?"

"That Willowby accused Mr. Lucas so he could get his hands on Lucas's land."

"How does the mayor figure in?"

"Willowby and him are good friends."

"I'll have to ride over there and talk to this Willowby," Fargo said.

"Tonight?"

Fargo thought of a luscious body in a pink robe. "No. I have somewhere else to be tonight."

"Goodness gracious, don't you ever rest?"

"I'll be back in the morning. In the meantime, think about any friends who might take your boy and the girl in until this is over."

"This is Troy's home. They should stay here."

"The marshal can't arrest you for hiding them if they're not here."

"I'll think about it."

Fargo stood and stretched. "This will all be over in a few days, one way or the other."

"Talk like that scares me."

"You said it yourself. Bascomb won't stop so long as he's breathing."

"But you can't just walk up to him and shoot him. It would make you a wanted man."

"I have to be careful," Fargo agreed.

"Besides, I don't hold with killing. Thou shalt not kill, Scripture says. If everybody believed that this world would be a better place."

Fargo stepped to the back door. "Keep this and your front door bolted and don't open them for anyone."

"What if a neighbor stops by?"

"Not anyone," Fargo stressed.

"I pray the Good Lord watches over you."

Fargo stepped out into the welcome cool of evening and over to the Ovaro. He reached up to grip the saddle horn and a shadow detached itself from the house. He had the Colt out and cocked and then realized who it was. "Are you trying to get shot?"

"I wanted a few words," Clyde said, and glanced at the back door. "Without Rosemary hearing."

"What's on your mind?"

"It's this Bascomb business," the farmer said. "I've been thinking on it and there's only one thing to do. It won't end so long as he's alive."

"We think alike," Fargo said.

"I've never shot anyone. I don't even know if I could. But

that's my boy upstairs. I care for him, Mr. Fargo. More than I can put into words. And I'll be damned if I'll let Mayor Bascomb do to him as they did to Steve Lucas."

"I'm working on a plan."

"I've seen this before, back east. The rich and the powerful lording it over ordinary folks like us. All we want is to be left to live our lives in peace. But they never let us, do they?"

Fargo had a long ride ahead but he was willing to hear the farmer out.

"It's one of the reasons I came west," Clyde said. "I thought that out here I could live free and not have anyone breathing down my neck." He frowned. "I reckon I should have known better."

"The world is full of Bascombs."

"Ain't it a shame."

Fargo climbed on the Ovaro, the saddle creaking under his weight. He lifted the reins.

"Where are you off to?" Clyde asked.

"To brush up on my ABCs," Fargo said.

10

The schoolmarm's house stood quiet under the stars. Fargo rode around to the rear so the Ovaro couldn't be seen from the road and tied the reins to the lilac bush. A curtain in the kitchen window moved and he saw the schoolmarm peer out. She opened the back door as he was raising his hand to knock.

"You again."

"Glad I came?"

"No." Susan had on a sheer blue dress that fell to her shoes. Lace rimmed her throat and tiny white buttons ran from her throat down between her breasts to her slender waist. All in all it was a look befitting a schoolteacher and yet there was a hint of something more in how the dress clung suggestively, and how when she moved, it rustled like silk.

"Mind if I come in?"

"Yes," she said, but she stepped aside and held the door open.

Fargo strolled by and on into the parlor. "Nice place you have, Miss Brubaker." He was sincere. Her furnishings had a cozy quality.

"Call me Susan, please. Can I get you something to drink?"

"Whiskey if you have any."

Susan crossed to a cabinet. She set a bottle on a small table and excused herself to fetch a glass.

Fargo sat on the settee. The room smelled of perfume and other pleasant scents. A vase held roses. On a wall was a painting of a mountain landscape.

"Here you are." Susan brought two glasses over and filled both halfway. She sat at the other end of the settee.

"To you and me," Fargo said, and held his glass out.

"You take a lot for granted."

"I saw your eyes the last time I was here. You were interested."

Susan laughed. "I granted that you're handsome. I wasn't throwing myself at you."

Fargo let the whiskey burn his gullet. She liked an expensive brand, not the cheap stuff.

"Nothing to say?"

"Did you hear about Troy Utley?"

Susan blinked. "No. What?"

"Your friend the marshal beat on him and broke his hand," Fargo related.

"I don't believe it."

"Ride over to the Utleys' tomorrow and see for yourself. He's busted up inside, too. Should be bedridden for a week or more."

"It must have been a deputy," Susan said. "Lloyd would never hurt a boy like that."

"Travers does whatever the mayor wants, and the mayor wants Troy to stay away from Joan."

Susan's foot commenced to jiggle up and down. "Is that why you came? To talk about how despicable our town leaders are?"

Fargo smiled. "You know damn well why I came."

The schoolmarm flushed scarlet and gulped more whiskey to cover her embarrassment. "You trouble me."

"I do?"

"You have an effect on me that I'm not entirely sure I like."

Fargo ran his eyes from her lips to her cleavage to the swell of her thighs under her dress. "You have an effect on me, too."

"There you go again." Susan drained her glass, rose and walked to the cabinet to refill it. As she poured she said over her shoulder, "I'll confess I have been thinking of you. Since your visit I can hardly get you out of my mind."

"Imagine that," Fargo said.

"Don't be so conceited. It's a compliment. I'm not attracted to very many men the way I'm attracted to you."

"Lucky me."

"Must you be so vulgar?" Susan sat back down. She swished the whiskey in her glass and said softly, "I prefer my gentleman callers to be more—" She stopped as if searching for the right word.

"Gentlemanly?"

"Yes. Exactly. I like men who are kind and considerate. With you it's like a duel."

Fargo extended his forefinger and lowered his thumb and said, "Bang."

"See? Why do I have the sense that secretly you are laughing at me?"

"People have a lot of foolish notions."

"That's no answer. How do you feel about me?"

"I'd like to feel you under me and see the look in your eyes when you spurt."

Susan's mouth fell open and she gasped. "No one has ever talked to me the way you do."

"You like it. I can tell."

"I do not," Susan said, but she trembled slightly and her foot jiggled faster.

"Try taking deep breaths."

"You are too smug by half," Susan declared, her eyes dancing with anger. "I suppose you are accustomed to women falling all over you."

"I've been with a few," Fargo answered. The truth was, if he had to tally them up, it would take a month of Sundays.

"Well, aren't you the great lover?"

"That's for you to decide, after."

Susan drank so fast, she gulped it. "I can't make up my mind about you. Part of me wants to throw you out of my house."

"And the other part?"

"The part of me that no schoolteacher should ever admit she has is intrigued by your naughty behavior."

Fargo chuckled. "I get you upstairs, I'll show you how naughty I can be."

"You push and you push," Susan said, but not angrily.

"Mostly I move in and out."

In the act of swallowing, Susan snorted and laughed and got whiskey on her chin and on her dress. "Look at what you made me do!"

"I'd like to make you do a whole lot more."

"Stop it." Susan emptied her second glass and got up and stepped to the cabinet.

"When you drink, you drink," Fargo said.

"What's that supposed to mean?"

"I'm still on my first."

"I'm not a lush, thank you very much." Susan returned and sat closer to him than she had the last two times. "Do you know a man named Willowby?"

"Ben Willowby? Yes, I teach his son. How in the world did he come up?"

"What's he like?"

Susan shook her head in bemusement. "You ask the strangest questions. He's a big man in Promise. Not as big as the mayor but he has a lot of influence."

"Enough to get a farmer killed for his land?"

"I don't like where this conversation is headed. You're spoiling the mood."

"My mood is just fine," Fargo said, and reaching across, he slid his hand behind her neck and pulled her to him and kissed her on the mouth. She didn't pull away, and she didn't slap him when he broke the kiss.

"Not bad but I've had better."

Fargo set his glass on the table and was turning when he heard hooves. "Expecting more company?"

"No." Susan appeared confused. She set her glass next to his and hurried to the window. "Oh God. What is *he* doing here?"

"Who?"

Susan rushed to the hall. "Stay there and I'll get rid of him."

Careful not to show himself, Fargo went to the window and peered out.

Marshal Travers was ambling toward the front door with a big smile on his face.

Fargo moved close to the hall so he could hear. He put his hand on the Colt.

There was a knock and the squeak of the door.

"Good evening, Lloyd. To what do I owe this unexpected visit?"

"Susie," Travers said. "Why so formal?"

"You took it into your head to pay me a visit out of the blue?"

"Hey, now. What's gotten into you? The last time I was here you were a lot friendlier." Travers laughed.

"The last time I invited you, if you'll recall. This time you've showed up on your own."

Uncertainty crept into the lawman's voice. "Are you going to stand there or let me in?"

"I don't think I will tonight, no."

"This is a hell of a note."

"I'm not your property, Lloyd. We're friends. You should be more considerate."

"What in hell are you talking about? We're a damn sight more than *friends* and you damn well know it."

"Watch your language."

Fargo grinned when the lawmen indulged in a streak of swearing worthy of an army sergeant.

"I mean it, Lloyd. I won't have talk like that. I'm the schoolmarm, after all. Those I associate with are expected to be as virtuous as I am."

"You? Virtuous?"

"Be careful, Lloyd. Be very careful."

"Have you been drinking?"

"No."

"I'd swear I smell whiskey on your breath."

"Whether I have or I haven't is entirely none of your affair. Now I'll thank you to leave. I have a lot of papers to grade."

"For pity's sake, Susie, is it your time of the month or something?"

"You really should work on your sweet talk. It leaves a lot to be desired."

"Are you mad about me not trusting you when Joan Bascomb and the Utley boy were here?"

"I'd almost forgotten about that. Thank you for reminding me."

"The mayor wanted her back at all costs."

"And you lick his boots for him."

"That's not fair."

"Good night, Lloyd."

"You're acting awful high and mighty for someone who couldn't get enough of me the last time I graced your bed."

The door slammed shut loud enough to break the hinges.

Fargo ran to the window and dared another look. The lawman was marching off in a huff, gesturing and venting his spleen to the empty air.

Susan came back, her dress rustling about her. "I'm sorry. As I told you before, some men seem to think that if a woman is nice to them, they own her."

"Not me," Fargo said.

"What makes you so different?"

"When I'm with a woman I have no interest in owning her. I just like to fuck."

The schoolmarm burst into peals of mirth that doubled her over. She laughed so long and so hard that when she finally stopped she said, "My sides hurt something awful."

"It wasn't that funny."

"You are the first man to ever use that word in my presence. A lot of them think it but they would never say it."

"I think it and I do it," Fargo said, and grinned. "Say when."

11

The schoolmarm was on her sixth whiskey. She held her liquor surprisingly well for someone who wasn't ever supposed to let hard spirits touch her lips. And they were luscious lips. The longer Fargo admired them, the more he wanted to taste them.

At the moment Susan was peering at him over the rim of her glass, her eyes alight with interest she was trying hard to pretend she didn't have. "I like my position here. It pays well. The students come to class clean and have good manners."

"Plus there's Lloyd."

"I'll thank you not to mention him again." Susan lowered her glass and smirked. "Besides, he's not more than a— How shall I put this? Extracurricular activity."

"What the hell is that?"

"Haven't you ever done something for the fun of it?"

Fargo ate her body with his eyes. "All the time."

Pink showed on Susan's cheeks as she finished her glass. "I need another."

Fargo decided she had stalled long enough. Putting his hand on her wrist, he slid over so their bodies brushed. "What you need isn't in a bottle."

"The things that come out of your mouth," Susan said, and giggled.

"It's the thing I'd like to put into them," Fargo replied.

"Like what?" she teasingly asked.

Fargo set his glass on the table at the end of the settee, turned, and covered his left breast with his hand. "This, for starters."

Susan gasped. "I'll thank you to behave," she said huskily.

"You'll thank me more if I don't." Fargo cupped her other breast and molded his mouth to hers. She resisted for all of three seconds. Then she hungrily ground against him. He had been right about her mouth; she kissed deliciously. He sucked on her tongue and she sucked on his and a tiny moan escaped her.

Fargo ran a hand through her silken hair and down over her shoulders to the small of her back, rubbing in small circles.

She cooed in delight.

He commenced to undo her buttons. There were so many, it annoyed him. He liked dresses that could be shed as easily as socks, not ones that took forever to get out of. While he pried, he kissed and licked her mouth, her throat, her ears. She responded with ardor.

At last the dress parted and Fargo slid a hand under her undergarments and cupped the real article. Her nipple was as hard as a tack. At the contact she arched her back. When he pinched her nipple and pulled, she sucked in a breath and said, "Yes, yes, like that."

Fargo fondled and caressed her mounds. His need climbed. His pants bulged. When she brazenly put a hand on him, he pressed her onto the settee.

"My goodness, you're a big one," Susan husked.

Fargo started shedding clothes. He got her dress off and her chemise and the rest. Finally she lay naked and panting. She was glorious. From the sheen of her hair to the ruby red

72

of her mouth to the fullness of her mounds with their rigid nipples to the flat of her belly and the velvet swell of her thighs, she was a living portrait of female perfection.

Fargo undid his gun belt and set it on the floor. He got his pants down and positioned himself, and didn't like it. The settee cushions were too thin. It was hard on his knees. Getting off, he pulled his pants back up and grabbed his gun belt and slung it over his shoulder.

"What are you doing?" Susan asked. "You haven't changed your mind, have you?"

"That'll be the day." Fargo slid his arms under her and lifted. "Any objections to using your bed?"

"None at all," Susan said, and tittered.

It was a long climb up the stairs. A lamp on the dresser cast the bedroom in a golden glow. He eased her onto the quilt, shed his gun belt and his boots and his pants, and climbed on the bed next to her. She welcomed him with open arms and open lips. They melted into one another and he devoted his hands to her thighs. She parted them wider. The heat her nether mound gave off when he cupped it was enough to set his fingers on fire. He parted her lips and ran a fingertip across her slit. Susan shivered and her eyelids fluttered and she groaned long and loud.

"More," she said. "More."

Fargo inserted a finger and her back became a bow. He inserted a second finger, and pumped, and she fused herself to him, her mouth clamped hotly to his. She wasn't one of those women who had the habit of lying flat on their backs like logs while the men did all the arousing; she stoked his flame as he stoked hers.

When her fingers enfolded him, down low, it was all Fargo could do not to explode. She traced his entire length and then cupped him.

"Magnificent," she breathed.

Fargo could say the same. Her body was exquisite. He pulled his fingers out and touched the tip of his member to her slit.

"Do it. Hurry."

To tease her, Fargo slid in fraction by fraction until he was wreathed in her satiny sheath. For a bit she was still except for the heaving of her bosom. He pumped his hips and suddenly she became a frenzied whirlwind of carnal desire. She locked her ankles behind his back and pumped.

The bed bounced. Fargo pulsed and rammed and felt his release building. He held off, though; he always liked for the woman to gush first and the schoolmarm didn't disappoint him. She was moving like a piston when her eyes grew wide and she cried out. Her fingernails dug into his shoulders and she gushed.

Fargo let himself go. For a while it was like an ocean tide of pleasure and then he was on his side next to her and the two of them were satiated and glistening with sweat.

"God, you're good," Susan said dreamily.

"Don't tell Lloyd."

"You mention his goddamn name one more time and I will by God shoot you."

"Such a mouth for a schoolmarm."

Susan laughed. "You have quite a mouth, yourself."

Fargo closed his eyes. Sleep tugged at him. It had been a long, eventful day. He drifted off. How long he'd slept when his eyes snapped open, he couldn't say, but he felt it hadn't been long. He lay there wondering what woke him. Then a floorboard in the hall creaked. Quickly, he slid off the far side of the bed and drew the Colt from his holster. Another creak confirmed someone was out there. Flattening, he swiftly dressed as quietly as possible. When he raised his head a revolver blasted and a slug nearly took off his ear. He responded with two rapid blasts, shooting into the wall near the barrel of the revolver that was poking past the jamb. Boots clomped, moving at a run, and he was up and around the bed as Susan sat upright and let out a yelp of fright.

"What's going on? Who are you shooting at?"

Fargo reached the top of the stairs in time to see the back of the person who had shot at him. The boots pounded into the parlor. He raced down and crouched at the bottom. "I know you're in there," he hollered, thinking the shooter might answer and give his position away, but the man was too smart. Or so he figured until he heard the thud of hooves. A glance at the front door showed it was still bolted. He ran into the parlor.

A curtain flapped in the breeze. The window had been raised. Fargo shut it and twisted the latch. Reloading as he walked, he returned to the bedroom.

Susan had her pink robe on and was donning fluffy slippers. "What was all that shooting about?" she anxiously asked. "Who was it?"

"If I say his name you'll shoot me," Fargo said.

"No!" Susan exclaimed.

"Yes."

"How did he get in?"

Fargo told her about the window.

"Damn. Sometimes I open them to let in fresh air and forget to latch them again. I'm sorry." She sounded sincere. "But how did he know you were in here?"

"He must have been suspicious when you wouldn't let him in," Fargo guessed. "Could be he nosed around and saw my horse."

"Oh God," Susan said. "He'll be mad as hell at me."

"Would he hurt you?"

Susan grinned. "Harm the schoolmarm? He'd be strung up so fast his head would swim."

Fargo didn't share her confidence. Travers was a town's worst nightmare: a lawman gone bad. Travers was in the pocket of the richest man in Promise; he'd gone along with hanging a man who didn't deserve it; and he'd beaten a boy for running off with the rich man's daughter. Now the coyote had snuck into the teacher's house and tried to murder him in the middle of the night. "You should keep a gun handy."

"I don't own one."

"I can lend you my rifle."

"Quit fretting. I tell you, Lloyd won't dare lay a finger on me."

"Come stay with the Utleys," Fargo suggested. "Until this is over."

"Will you listen to yourself?" Susan shook her head. "I'm a grown woman. I can take care of myself. And I have a perfectly fine house of my own."

Fargo saw there was no persuading her. "You can get word to me through them if you have to." He hitched at his gun belt.

"You're leaving?"

"Afraid so."

Susan came over and pressed herself against him. "That's a shame. I was hoping for a second helping."

"I'll be back," Fargo said. He'd like a second taste, himself. He kissed her and she went with him to the kitchen and over to the back door.

"Watch your back, handsome. I daresay Lloyd and the mayor will have it in for you."

"They already do." Fargo slipped out into the cool of night. Once on the Ovaro he rode in ever-wider circles to be sure the lawman was indeed gone. Then he headed for the Utley farm.

The ride gave him time to think. He was one man against a devil with more money than Midas and a tin star who used his badge as a license to hurt and kill. They could easily brand him a wanted man and put a price on his head, if they hadn't already. He needed to show the people of Promise what their so-called leaders were like, as much for his sake as for the Utleys. Then there was Rosemary and her husband. They needed public sentiment on their side or they might wind up like Steve Lucas.

The ride was peaceful. The stars overhead, the dull drum of hooves and the soft breeze about lulled him into dozing off in the saddle.

A light glowed in a front window of the farmhouse but Fargo didn't go in. At that hour they were all asleep and he didn't care to wake them.

He spread out his blankets in the barn and slept with the Colt in one hand and his other hand on the Henry.

Fargo was up at first light. He saddled the Ovaro and led the stallion around to the back door. Inside, a pot clinked. Rosemary, no doubt. He paused with his hand on the latch and gazed to the east at the brightening sky. An idea had come to him. After breakfast he would start his campaign to rid Promise of its bad apples. Whether it worked or it didn't, one thing was for certain—blood would be spilled.

12

The Willowby farm was grander than the Utleys'. The farmhouse was three times as big and the barn gigantic. There were more outbuildings and a large corral. But the crops were in poor shape. Lack of water was the problem; where they should have been green, they were turning brown and withering.

Fargo rode up to the house. A few trees provided shade and under one of them sat a skinny woman in a dress and an apron who was busy shucking peas. She looked up and went on shucking as he drew rein and climbed down. "Morning, ma'am."

"We don't like strangers on our place, mister," she said in a reedy voice. "Get back on your horse and scat."

Fargo took an instant dislike to her. She had all the warmth of a block of ice. "Would you be Mrs. Willowby?"

"Didn't you hear me?"

"I need to speak to your husband."

"What do you need to see Dorn about?"

"This and that," Fargo said.

She stopped shucking and swiped at a strand of hair that had fallen over her bony face. "You are beginning to aggravate me."

"Where is he?"

The woman threw back her head and put the same hand to her mouth and yelled, "Brian! Thad! Get out here!"

Two young men came out of the barn. They wore home-spun and had the bodies of bulls. One had sandy hair, like the woman in the chair. The other's hair was black. They cast barbed looks at Fargo.

"What do you need, Ma?"

Mrs. Willowby stabbed a thin finger at Fargo. "This here he-goat is uppity. I'd like him to leave and I'd like him to leave now."

"You should go when our ma says to," the other son said.

"Don't waste words on him, Thad," Mrs. Willowby said. "Throw him off our property."

Thad balled his fists and turned to Fargo with flint in his eyes. "Yes, Ma." He walked up to Fargo and glared down at him. "Get on your horse."

"All I want is to talk to your pa," Fargo said.

"He's not here," said the dark-haired one, Brian. "He's off digging irrigation ditches from the Lucas farm to—"

"Hush, boy," Mrs. Willowby cut him off. "He's doesn't need to know that."

Thad hadn't stopped glaring. "You best get on that horse, mister, or we'll pound you."

"A shame what happened to Lucas," Fargo said.

Mrs. Willowby had bent to her pail of peas, but stopped. "How's that, mister?"

"Your husband claimed Lucas stole a cow just so you could get your hands on Lucas's land."

"I don't know what in hell you're talking about."

"Did Mayor Bascomb agree to hang Lucas for money or out of the goodness of his heart?"

"Boys," Mrs. Willowby said. "Break every bone in this son of a bitch's body."

"Yes, Ma," Thad said, and swung.

Fargo ducked and slammed a fist into the younger man's

gut. It had no effect. Sidestepping, he rammed a cross to the jaw. It had less. The other boy, Brian, came at Fargo from the side and he retreated. Both came after him. That neither was armed made it harder. He couldn't just shoot them, as much as he might like to.

"Bust him good, boys!" Mrs. Willowby yipped.

They came at him from two sides. Fargo turned to ward off Thad and Brian punched him low in the back. He turned to counter Brian and Thad caught him in the ribs. He retreated farther and they leaped at him, their fists poised. He pretended to trip and shifted so they didn't see him draw. Thad reared over him and he smashed the Colt against Thad's right knee. Bellowing in rage and pain, Thad staggered. Brian glanced at his brother and Fargo raked him across the kneecap.

Both brothers bent and clutched their legs.

Fargo trained the Colt on them. "That'll be enough."

"Damn you!" Thad fumed.

"You don't fight fair!" Brian said.

Fargo warily circled to the Ovaro.

The mother's whole skinny body was twitching, she was so mad. "You hurt my boys, you bastard."

"What did you expect?" Fargo snagged the reins. "If there's a next time I won't go easy on them." He hooked his boot in the stirrup and pulled himself up.

"Get off our property and stay off," Mrs. Willowby said. "And leave my husband be, you hear? He told the truth about our cow."

"Like hell he did."

"He did so, mister!" Thad declared.

Brian went on rubbing his knee.

Fargo reined the Ovaro around but twisted so he could cover them as he rode off.

"You let my husband be, you hear!" Mrs. Willowby said again. "It won't do you any good, anyhow. Lucas is dead and his farm is ours."

Holstering the Colt, Fargo brought the stallion to a trot.

That hadn't gone well. Now he had three more enemies to add to the growing list.

The Lucas place was to the east. He had gone a few miles when he heard voices and the clink of metal. Reining into a wash, he followed it near enough that when he rose in the stirrups, he could see the source.

A party of eight men was busy digging a ditch. Picks bit into the earth. Shovels pumped dirt. A buckboard and several horses were nearby. On the seat sat a man who was an older image of Brian. He had a rifle.

Fargo fought shy of them, for now. In half an hour he came on to a tidy farmhouse nestled in a vale of green. Fed by a creek, a pond lay broad and blue under the sun. In front of the house sat a covered wagon. A middle-aged woman and a boy of fifteen or so were bringing furniture and possessions out of the house and piling them in the bed. They stopped and uneasily regarded him as he rode up. As he stopped, the boy took a few steps, scowling in anger.

"We're loading as fast as we can! Go and tell Willowby to leave us be."

The woman came to the boy's side. She reminded Fargo of a younger Rosemary. "He doesn't look like one of them," she said. "They don't wear buckskins."

"You're Mrs. Lucas?" Fargo said.

The woman nodded, weariness and sorrow on her kindly face. "This is my son, James."

"Why are you leaving?"

It was James who answered. "What else could we do when the bank threatened to take our land?"

Fargo gazed out over the green fields of corn and the oats and the vegetables that could be harvested. "You can't make ends meet with a farm like this?"

"We could except for the paper they say my husband signed," Mrs. Lucas said.

"I bet he never did, Ma," James said bitterly.

"What paper?" Fargo asked.

Again it was the boy who replied. "The bank has it. They claim my pa borrowed more money. For improvements, the banker said. Ma and me could have made the old payments. But the new payments are so high, Ma had no choice but to sell."

"To Dorn Willowby."

"For pennies on the dollar," Mrs. Lucas said.

Fargo had a thought. "Tell me. Who owns the bank in Promise?"

"Harry Bascomb. He's also the mayor."

"I'll be damned," Fargo said. Banker *and* mayor *and* judge. Bascomb was the king of the roost and could rule as he saw fit.

"Mister?" Mrs. Lucas said.

"I'm sorry for you, ma'am."

"Who are you?"

In light of what Fargo had in mind, he figured the fewer who knew his name, the wiser it was. "Nobody important."

"You're friendly, and for that I thank you."

"I'll be around a few days yet. You might want to stay. Could be there will be a new banker."

"Wouldn't help us none," she said. "I had to sign the place away so it was legal. Mr. Willowby insisted."

"Legal," Fargo said, and laughed.

James happened to be facing to the west, and went stiff with alarm. "Ma! Look who's coming."

There were two of them. They had been at the ditch and their clothes were smeared with dirt. They slowed at pistol distance and came on slowly. Only one wore a sidearm. The other had a rifle.

"Who are you, mister, and what are you doing here?" the one with the sidearm demanded.

Mrs. Lucas intervened. "He's just passing through, Mr. Keller. No need to act so mean."

Keller didn't take his eyes off Fargo. "Mr. Willowby sent us to check on how you and the boy are coming along. He wants you out of here by sunset."

"Don't call me a boy," James said.

"We'll be out," Mrs. Lucas said.

"You'd better be," Keller told them.

Fargo wheeled the Ovaro so he faced the pair and rested his hand on his Colt. "I need an excuse."

"You need what?" the man with the rifle said.

"An excuse to get close to Willowby. You two will do real nice."

"What in hell are you talking about? Why would we take you to see him? We don't know who you are."

"No one here does," Fargo said.

"You're making no sense," Keller said.

"I'd like to let your boss know how I feel about hanging a man over a cow he never stole," Fargo said.

The two men looked at each other.

"Lucas was really hung over his water," Fargo went on. "But I reckon you peckerwoods already know that, don't you?"

"Mister, you're not even a little funny," Keller said.

"How far up Bascomb's ass does Willowby have his nose?" Fargo asked.

"I'm warning you."

"How far up Willowby's ass do you two have yours?"

"That does it," said the man with the rifle as he began to level it.

Fargo shot him in the head. Keller stabbed for his six-shooter and Fargo shot him, too, between the eyes. In the sudden silence the two bodies thudded to the ground.

"Land of Goshen!" Mrs. Lucas exclaimed.

"Did you see that, Ma?" James marveled.

Fargo climbed down. He reloaded, then went through the pockets of the dead men and came up with seven dollars and forty cents. He checked their saddlebags, too, and found another three dollars. "For you," he said, holding it out to the widow. "It's not much but it might help."

"I couldn't take that."

"Ma!" James said.

"I'd feel tainted, son."

Fargo nodded at the bodies. "They rode for the man who had your husband hung and stole your land out from under you with the help of his friend the mayor."

"You provoked them. I saw it."

Fargo took her hand and placed the money in her palm. She didn't drop it or give it back. "Ma'am, I've just begun to provoke."

13

Willowby was off the wagon seat and standing near the ditch talking to several others when Fargo rode up leading the horses with the dead men slung over their saddles. One of the diggers said something and Willowby turned. The others stopped digging to stare.

Fargo came to a stop and smiled and said, "I believe these belong to you."

Willowby was a big man gone to paunch. He had remarkably pale skin for a farmer, and close set eyes. His lips were the size of middling pickles, and when he scowled, as he did now, they seemed to cover half his face. "What the hell?" He stepped to the horses and put a hand on Keller's back. "Who did this?"

"They were shot," Fargo said. He was watching the others without being obvious. Only two wore revolvers and neither had made a move to draw.

"I can see that," Willowby said curtly. "What I want to know is why? And who the hell are you?"

"I'm the gent who did you a favor and brought them back," Fargo said.

"I'm obliged, mister. But I'm still waiting to hear the particulars. I sent them to check on a woman and her boy, the Lucases, and now they're dead. It doesn't make any sense."

"Maybe it was the boy who shot them," a digger said.

"They say he's a good hunter," said another. "He can handle a rifle real good."

"They were shot with a pistol," Fargo said.

"How do you know?" Willowby asked.

"I was there."

"Why didn't you say so?" Willowby stepped up to the Ovaro. "Tell me about it. Every detail."

"There was a man at the farm—"

"Did you get a good look at him?" Willowby interrupted. "What was he like?"

"He told your men that you stole the farm out from under the Lucases."

"What?"

"He said you had the father hung on a trumped-up charge."

"What?"

"He said you did it because your farm is dying. You need more water and figured to help yourself to theirs."

"This man said all that?"

Fargo nodded. "He said you're in cahoots with the mayor and the marshal, and the three of you put together aren't worth a gob of spit."

Willowby sputtered and stamped a foot like a riled buffalo. "Lies. All lies. Describe this man to me. I'm going after him."

"He's about my height," Fargo said.

"Yes."

"And about my weight."

"Yes. Yes."

"And he wear buckskins and a white hat and a red bandanna," Fargo said.

"Mister, you've just described yourself—" Willowby stopped. He had it now, and a hint of fear crept into his tone.

"Hold on. You shot them?"

"Dead as dead can be."

"And it was you who said all that about me stealing the Lucas farm?"

"I cannot tell a lie," Fargo lied.

"Why, you've committed murder."

"So did you, at the end of a rope."

Willowby took a step back. "Lucas was arrested and tried and convicted. I wasn't the judge. I didn't sentence him."

"A rigged trial," Fargo said, "with your friend Bascomb presiding. You might as well have pointed a gun at Lucas and pulled the trigger."

Willowby glanced at Fargo's Colt and wet his lips. "What was Lucas to you?"

"Never met the man."

"Then why are you acting as if you have to avenge him?" Willowby asked in confusion.

"I'm stirring up the hornet's nest and you're one of the hornets."

Willowby looked at the men beside him and those in the ditch. "Is it me or is he touched in the head?"

"Don't look at me," said a man with a shovel. "You hired me to dig. I don't want any part of this other."

"Are you heeled?" Fargo asked. Willowby wasn't wearing a six-shooter but there was always the chance he had a hideout.

"I am not," Willowby declared, and held his arms out from his sides. "You can search me if you want. But if you shoot me, you'll be gunning down an unarmed man."

"The man you had hung wasn't armed."

Beads of sweat speckled Willowby's face. "I tell you he stole that cow."

Fargo looked at the pair who had gun belts. "How about

you two? Care to swap lead? Then I can shoot him in the head and say it was a mistake."

"You're insane," Willowby said. He jabbed a finger at the other two. "Keep your hands away from your hardware—you hear me? You're not to give this lunatic an excuse."

"You are no fun," Fargo said.

"I'm going to report you to the marshal," Willowby huffed. "I'll take those dead men in and have you charged with murder."

"I'd be grateful."

"Stark raving insane," Willowby said.

"Give the mayor a message for me while you're at it."

"What message?"

Fargo drew and shot Dorn Willowby in the thigh. Willowby shrieked and collapsed. The others turned to stone. Willowby thrashed and groaned and cried out and eventually subsided in a weak heap.

"You shot me, you bastard."

"Only once," Fargo said, and shot him again, in the other leg. He sat and waited for the blubbering and whimpering to stop, his Colt trained on the others.

Willowby was on his back, red puddles under each leg.

"Tell Bascomb that he isn't the only one who can play God," Fargo said.

His face contorted in pain, tears streaking his cheeks, Willowby said, "I'll be on crutches for a year."

"If you're still here a week from now you won't have to worry about crutches," Fargo said.

"What are you saying? You can't just drive a man from his home and his land."

"You're driving the Lucases." Fargo cocked the Colt and pointed it at Willowby's head.

"No!" Willow screeched, flinging out his bloody hands.

Fargo turned to the men. "Get him to town. And one of you give my regards to the mayor and ask him if he'll be able to get the bloodstains out of his floor."

"Mister, you are plumb loco."

"No," Fargo said. "I'm mad." He reined around and brought the Ovaro to a gallop, watching over his shoulder until he was out of range. He had stirred things up nicely, he thought. Now he needed to ensure that those who might be hurt by his stirring weren't.

The gray of twilight was darkening the Utley farm when he got there. It was suppertime, and smoke curled from the stone chimney.

Fargo went around to the back. He knocked, and Joan opened the door. She had an apron on and looked terribly tired. Smiling wanly, she rose onto her toes and kissed him on the cheek.

"What was that for?"

"Saving me from my father."

"You're not safe yet."

Rosemary was at the stove. A pot was boiling and thick slabs of meat simmered in a frying pan. She wiped her hands on her apron and said, "I'm relieved to see you are in one piece. I've been worried you would get into more trouble."

"I tried my best." Fargo sat at the table. Joan brought him a cup and saucer and filled it with coffee without being asked. She brought over the sugar and cream and a spoon. "Thank you, little one."

"I'm almost a woman, I'll have you know."

Fargo usually took his coffee black but he spooned two heaping portions of sugar and added cream and stirred. "How's your boy?" he asked Rosemary.

"Coming along." She turned a steak over. "He wants to get out of bed but I won't let him."

"You might have to," Fargo said.

"Why?"

"By this time tomorrow I expect the marshal to show up," Fargo related. "Is there anyone you can hide out with until this is over?"

"We have a few friends who might help," Rosemary said.

Fargo remembered his encounter in the hills with the two hunters. "Would one of those friends happen to be Wilt Flanders?"

"It would," Rosemary confirmed. "His wife, Martha, is a dear. How would you know him?"

"We've met," was all Fargo would say.

"Clyde won't like leaving any more than I do," Rosemary said. "This is our home. He'll defend it with his life if he has to."

"Do you want it to come to that?"

"No," Rosemary said, and shook her head. "No, I assuredly do not."

"After we eat, talk to him," Fargo advised. "Convince him that breathing is better than not breathing." The aroma of the steak made his mouth water. He realized he hadn't eaten since the day before.

Joan brought bread from the cupboard and a plate of butter. "I hate my father," she said out of the blue.

"I don't blame you."

"I mean it," Joan said. "After what he had the doctor do to me, I hate him more than ever. I hate him enough that I want him dead."

"Now, now," Rosemary said.

"I mean it."

"Don't let your hate sour your soul," Rosemary said. "It can make you do things you shouldn't."

Joan wasn't listening. "As soon as Troy is able we should leave for Oregon and never come back."

"Never?" Rosemary said.

"Oh, we could sneak back to visit now and then, just so long as my father didn't know. But it would be easier if he wasn't around."

"You kill him, it will haunt you forever."

"He haunts me now," Joan said.

Just then Clyde hurried into the kitchen toting his shotgun. "Did any of you hear anything?"

"Like what?" Rosemary asked.

"Horses," Clyde said.

"No."

Clyde walked to a window. "I thought for sure I heard some but when I looked out of the bedroom I didn't see anyone."

"Maybe it was Mr. Fargo's you heard," Rosemary said. "He got here a short while ago."

"No. There was more than one and they were riding hard."

Fargo put down his cup and started to stand. "I'll go outside and check."

Clyde turned and nodded—and the window exploded in a shower of glass and lead.

14

Clyde cried out as his right shoulder erupted in a spray of blood. Joan screamed. Rosemary stood rooted in horror. Fargo was the only one who flattened, and when the fusillade ended, he drew his Colt and caught Clyde as the farmer keeled forward. Quickly taking him into the hallway, he laid Clyde down and said to Rosemary, "Tend to him." To Joan he barked, "Get upstairs and stay with Troy. Keep him in bed." Then he dashed to the window.

The sun had set. In the dark figures moved—how many, Fargo couldn't say. A lot of the glass had been shot out and through the holes came furtive sounds. He glanced at the Ovaro and wanted to kick himself for leaving his rifle in the saddle scabbard.

Staying low, Fargo ran to Rosemary and her husband. Clyde was gritting his teeth as she probed at the wound. There was a lot of blood. "How is he?"

"It went clean through," she said. "If I can stop the bleeding he should be all right."

"Shot me in my own home!" Clyde declared through clenched teeth. "They didn't give me a chance to defend myself. The yellow dogs."

"Hush," Rosemary said. "Save your strength."

"Don't go anywhere near the windows," Fargo cautioned her, and returned to the kitchen. The men outside were still moving around. Surrounding the farmhouse, he reckoned. Apparently he had guessed wrong about the marshal not showing up until the next day.

From out of the dark came a bellow. "You hear me in there? This is Mayor Bascomb."

"Son of a bitch," Fargo said.

"That was to get your attention. Now that I have it, I want you to listen, and listen good."

Fargo probed the night in the direction the voice was coming from. One shot, and he could end this.

"Stranger!" Bascomb shouted. "The one in buckskins! I know you're in there so answer me."

"I hear you," Fargo yelled.

"I have men on all sides," Bascomb declared. "Try to get away and we'll gun you down."

"Step out where I can see you and I'll do the same," Fargo responded.

"I want my daughter!" Bascomb demanded. "I know you brought her here. We followed your trail from my house. Send her out to me."

Fargo frowned. He hadn't counted on Bascomb having a tracker. "What if she doesn't want to?"

"I'll give her five minutes. If she hasn't come out by then there will be hell to pay."

Fargo turned to go upstairs and talk to Joan but there was no need. She entered the kitchen. Troy was with her; she was holding his arm to support him. "I told you to keep him in bed."

"He wouldn't listen," she said in exasperation.

"She told me my pa was shot," Troy said. His face was still badly swollen and discolored. Turning to his parents, he put his hand on his father's good shoulder. "They'll pay for this, Pa. Wait and see."

Fargo was more interested in what the girl was going to do. "You heard your father?"

Joan nodded. "I'll have to go out. There's no telling what he'll do if I don't."

"The one thing he won't do is turn the house into a sieve while you're inside," Fargo said. "It's better for us and for you if you stay."

"I don't know," Joan said uncertainly.

"Buy us some time," Fargo said. "Talk to him."

Joan nodded. She went near the window and seemed to wrestle with herself and then called out, "Father! It's me. Can you hear me?"

"Joan! Are you all right, child?" came the reply.

"Stop calling me that. I'm not your little girl anymore. Try to treat me with respect."

"What are you talking about? There is no one in this world I hold more dear."

"Yet you had the doctor drug me," Joan angrily shouted. "You kept me at our country house against my will."

"It was for your own good."

Joan was growing madder. "How dare you? What gives you the right to treat me that way? I'm not five years old anymore. When will you realize that?"

"This is hardly the time or the place for us to discuss this," Bascomb said. "Come outside and I'll forgive you for what you've done and we can start over."

"You're unbelievable," Joan said.

"I'm your father, and I care for you, and I do what is in your best interest whether you see it is or not. When you're older you'll thank me."

"I hate you."

"You don't mean that."

"I hate you. I hate you. I hate you."

"Listen to yourself. You keep saying you're not a little girl yet that's exactly what you sound like." Bascomb paused. "Come out of there, Joan. Please."

"No. You'll just have me drugged again and keep me locked away."

"What if I give you my word I won't?"

"I don't trust you."

"When have I ever lied to you?"

Joan didn't say anything.

"Come out," Bascomb said again. "If you're worried about the Utleys, I won't harm them. I'll leave them for the marshal."

"The marshal?" Joan said.

"They're lawbreakers. The boy abducted you. His parents have harbored him. They'll be arrested and charged and go on trial for their crimes."

"With you as the judge."

"I was duly appointed. And you know I'll be fair in my judgment."

"Like you were with Mr. Lucas?"

Bascomb didn't have a reply to that. Half a minute went by before he said, "I repeat. I give you my word the Utleys won't be harmed."

"What about—" Joan glanced at Fargo. "I just realized I don't know your name."

"What about who?" Bascomb shouted. "That buckskin-clad desperado who came to our house and attacked two deputies and killed our stableman? I've given orders he's to be shot on sight. In the unlikely event he's taken alive, he'll be hung."

"You call that justice?"

"He's a killer, child."

"So are you."

Fargo thought he heard a sigh.

"I'm trying to be reasonable. Can't you at least meet me halfway? Come on out and we'll talk some more. My men won't shoot. I promise."

"No."

"I'm losing my patience."

"Lose it all you want," Joan told him. "But keep this in mind." She paused. "If you send your men in after me, I'll shoot them."

"This is outrageous behavior."

"Be that as it may, you're not taking me alive. I want you to leave, Father. Take your men and go."

"That's not going to happen, child."

"Then we have nothing more to say to each other."

Bascomb called her name several times but Joan didn't answer. She bowed her head, tears glistening on her cheeks, and trembled.

"I really do hate him."

Fargo checked on the Ovaro. So far Bascomb and his men had left it alone but there was no telling what they would do should things get worse.

Joan turned and stared at the Utleys. Rosemary was bandaging Clyde. Troy sat slumped against the wall, wincing in pain. "What are we going to do?"

"We'll figure something out."

"Look at them. They're sweet, dear, kind people." Joan gave a soft sob. "This is my fault. I've brought this down on their heads."

"Bullshit."

Joan looked at him. "I beg your pardon."

"Your father is to blame. Him and no one else. He'll do whatever it takes to keep you under his thumb."

Dabbing at her eyes, Joan nodded. "Yes. Of course you're

right. I'm sorry. It's just—" Her eyes misted again. "I can't stand to see people I care for hurt."

"Go be with Troy," Fargo suggested, and when she walked over, he leaned against the wall to ponder. Bascomb didn't strike him as the patient kind. Sooner or later, and more likely sooner, Bascomb would get tired of waiting for Joan to give in and try to take her by force. He had to come up with something before then.

Leaving the window, Fargo went on a circuit of the house; upstairs, downstairs, every room from top to bottom. Other than the front and back doors, the only way out was through the ground floor windows. All of which faced open areas of the yard. They wouldn't get ten feet without being spotted. He returned to the kitchen.

Clyde was at the table, drinking water. Rosemary had wiped up the blood and bundled the bloody towels and was placing them in the sink. Joan and Troy were by the counter, whispering.

"Where have you been?" Rosemary asked.

"Trying to figure a way out," Fargo said.

"There's the root cellar," Clyde said. "You can go through it to the storm door. The bushes outside are so overgrown, they might not know it's there."

"What root cellar?" Fargo hadn't seen sign of one.

"Show him, Rosemary."

She opened the pantry and pointed at a trapdoor in the floor.

Fargo knelt and opened it. A dank odor rose from a pit of ink.

"We keep the usual down there," Rosemary said. "Preserves. Jerked meat. Potatoes and such."

"Hold a lamp for me."

Rosemary brought one over. Its glow revealed a short flight of steps. Fargo descended into an oval pit barely high enough for him to stand. Shelves lined the sides. The floor was dirt. He moved past the shelves to a door set at a low angle to the ground. Storm doors were common on farmhouses on the plains but not so common this far north. He put his shoulder to it and pushed. Thankfully, the hinges didn't creak. He raised it enough to poke his head out and saw what Clyde had been talking about. Several large bushes hid the storm door from view. He closed the door and went back up to the kitchen.

"Are your horses in the corral?"

"Except the plow horse. It's in the barn."

Fargo did some fast thinking. "I'm going out. I won't be gone long."

"What if they spot you?" Rosemary said. "That awful Harry Bascomb said they will shoot you on sight."

"I'll be careful. No matter what you hear, no one is to come after me. Is that understood?" Fargo looked at each of them and they nodded. "Good." Descending again, he crossed to the storm door and quietly opened it all the way, holding on to the edge so it wouldn't bump. In a crouch he moved through the bushes to the grass. To his right the ground was open, save for a few trees. To his left was the vegetable garden. Beyond it, the squat shape of the barn and the corral.

Fargo tensed. A shadow was moving across the yard. He raised the Colt but the man was only circling the house and watching the windows. Fargo let him go by. Retreating to the storm door, he closed it after him and in a few moments was back in the kitchen. The others were at the table.

"Well?" Clyde said. "What do you think?"

"As soon as you're able, we'll try."

"I'm able now."

"No, he's not," Rosemary said. "He's lost too much blood. He's weak yet."

"We'll wait an hour or so," Fargo said, hoping Bascomb's patience would last that long.

"What do you have in mind?" Joan asked.

Fargo explained, ending with, "By daylight we'll be miles away. We'll head for the Flanders farm and you can lie low."

"What about you?"

"I have a few scores to settle."

"Don't let my father get his hands on you," Joan said. "He can be vicious."

"He's not the only one," Fargo said.

15

Rosemary made soup. She chopped up carrots and potatoes and cut up the meat and put all of it, along with spoonfuls of flour, into the pot. When it was boiling she had everyone sit at the table and brought over bowls filled to the brim. Clyde said he wasn't hungry but she told him that he needed to eat to get his strength up. He ended up having two bowls.

So did Fargo. They had a long night ahead and he needed to keep *his* strength up.

Troy's jaw was so sore and swollen that he chewed in slow motion and grimaced with every bite. But he got enough soup down to restore some color.

They were almost done when the thunder of hooves warned them that more riders had arrived. There was a commotion outside, harsh voices and an argument.

"I wonder what that's about," Rosemary said.

Hardly were the words out of her mouth than someone pounded on the back door. Fargo rose out of his chair with his Colt in his hand. He motioned for the others to retreat into the hallway and called out, "Who is it?"

"Marshal Travers. Open up. I'm not armed."

"Keep your hands where I can see them," Fargo said as he threw the bolt and backpedaled.

The lawman stayed in the doorway. His holster was empty

and he held his arms out in front of him, his palms toward Fargo. "I want to talk."

"You just got here?"

Travers nodded. "I passed Dorn Willowby being brought into town in a buckboard. He says you shot him in both legs after killing two of his men."

"They went for their hardware first."

"Maybe so," Travers said, "but I still have to arrest you. Make this easy and hand over your six-shooter and I give you my word you won't be harmed."

"You and the mayor," Fargo said.

"What about us?"

"You tried to backshoot me at the schoolmarm's, you son of a bitch."

Travers must have been good at poker. "I don't know what you're talking about," he said without a change of expression.

"It will be a cold day in hell before I give you my Colt," Fargo said.

"This will get ugly if you don't."

"This will get ugly anyway."

Travers swore under his breath. "I can see I won't get anywhere with you. What happens next is on your head, not mine." He gazed past Fargo at the others. "How about the rest of you? Do you want to give up now or draw this out?"

"You're a miserable lawman, Lloyd Travers," Rosemary said. "I don't mind telling you so to your face."

"I'll take that as a no." Travers focused on Joan. "How about you, girl? Your pa is willing to forgive and forget. He'll welcome you back with open arms."

"And put me in shackles or have me drugged." Joan shook her head. "I'm with Buckskin, there. It will be a cold day in hell."

"Idiots," Travers said in disgust. He turned to go but glanced at Fargo. "That reminds me. Who *are* you?"

"You don't know?"

"How the hell would I? You haven't told anyone. I want to know who you are."

Fargo laughed.

"Fine. You think you're so clever. But in a short while you'll find out you're not."

"Close the door behind you."

Travers made as if to slam it but glanced at the Colt and shut it quietly.

Fargo went to the window and saw the lawman melt into the darkness. "We can't wait any longer. We have to go."

The others came into the kitchen and Rosemary joined him at the window. "Why the hurry?"

"Travers can't be so stupid as to think I'd give up."

"What other purpose could he have for talking to us?" Rosemary asked, and answered her own question. "Or was it to see how many are in the house?"

"And where we were," Fargo said.

"He wouldn't do that unless they were about to rush us," Rosemary deduced.

"We think alike. Bring the others." Fargo hurried into the pantry and raised the trapdoor. The four followed him down. Rosemary insisted on helping Clyde, who kept trying to push her hand away until finally she smacked his arm and told him to behave.

At the storm door, Fargo turned. Enough light filtered down from the kitchen to illuminate their worried faces. "Once you're out, crawl to the end of the vegetable patch and wait there."

"What will you be doing?" Troy asked.

"Keeping watch. Anyone spots us, anyone shoots at us,

I'll deal with them." Fargo nodded at Joan. "Close the pantry door. It will be pitch-black until you're outside. I'll help each of you out."

Rosemary's hand found his. "We can't thank you enough. You're a marvelous man."

"Hell," Fargo said. "They took my horse. It made me mad."

"That's all this is for you? Revenge?"

"It's enough." Fargo put his shoulder to the storm door. "Be as quiet as you can be." He pushed and held on until the door was all the way open. Reaching behind him, he snagged Rosemary's sleeve. She started to climb and tripped and he held her elbow to steady her.

"Sorry," she whispered in his ear.

Fargo assisted her out. She eased onto her hands and knees and then onto her belly and crawled toward the vegetable garden. He reached down and got hold of Clyde. The old farmer didn't swat at him as he had at his wife. Favoring his wounded shoulder, Clyde flattened and snaked after her. Troy was next. Then Joan emerged, her eyes luminous in the starlight. She smiled and dropped and crawled.

Fargo reached out with his senses. As near as he could tell, the men ringing the farmhouse were forty or fifty feet away. He started to sink down and caught movement out of the corner of his eye. A man was making another circuit of the house. Only this one was closer and would pass within a few feet of the bushes and practically on top of the Utleys and Joan.

Fargo hugged the ground. The man was looking at the house and not down. Firming his grip on the Colt, Fargo waited until his quarry was almost within reach, and sprang. The man spun and opened his mouth to cry out.

The fleshy thwack of the Colt's barrel as it slammed into the man's head was much too loud for Fargo's liking. Fortunately a second blow wasn't needed. The man melted to the grass.

Fargo crawled to catch up with the others. They had stopped when the man appeared. Now they were on the move again. Rosemary was the first to come to the end of the vegetable garden. She did as he had told her and waited.

Fargo went past all four of them. Twenty feet away was the outhouse. Forty feet past that, the barn. Bending, he whispered to Rosemary. "One at a time. Stay low and move as fast as you can. Wait behind the outhouse for me. Pass it on."

At the rear of the farmhouse Harry Bascomb unexpectedly gave a holler. "Joan! I want to talk to you!"

"Oh God," Joan whispered. "Not now."

"Did you hear me in there? I'm giving you one last chance to come out of your own free will."

Fargo detected movement. The men who had surrounded the house were moving toward the front and the back—and away from the garden and the outhouse and the barn. "Change of plans," he whispered over his shoulder. "When I stand up, run for the outhouse."

"All of us?" Rosemary asked.

"Together," Fargo confirmed. It was now or never; Travers was marshaling his men to attack the house.

"Joan!" the mayor bellowed. "I'm growing tired of your silliness."

Fargo rose and ran. No shouts challenged him. No shots boomed. He reached the outhouse and turned to protect the others. As soon as they were at his side, he said, "On to the barn."

"They'll see us," Clyde said.

"Maybe not." Fargo ran. He was trusting in luck more than anything. The marshal's men had no reason to suspect they weren't in the house.

"Joan!" Mayor Bascomb roared. "Enough is enough. Answer me this instant."

Fargo raced around the side of the barn and nearly collided with a horse tied to the corral. It was but one of nearly twenty that belonged to the mayor's men and the marshal's posse. All were saddled and ready to ride. "Help yourselves," he whispered.

"I'm no horse thief," Rosemary said. "I'll ride my own animal." She hustled to the gate, her husband at her heels.

"I'm not particular," Joan said, and picked one.

Troy was a chip off the parental blocks. "I won't steal, either," he said, and went into the corral after his own.

When the four of them were in their saddles and ready, Fargo gave his final instructions. "Ride like hell for the Flanders farm. Don't stop for anything."

"What about you?" Joan asked.

"I'm not coming."

"What on earth not?" Rosemary demanded.

"I can buy you time," Fargo said. Plus, there was the Ovaro; he wasn't leaving without it. "Skedaddle while you can." He turned Rosemary's animal and smacked it and off it went. Clyde and Troy were quick to file after her but Joan hesitated.

"Please be careful. We won't last long if anything happens to you."

"Look after the others," Fargo said, and gave her horse a smack, as well. He stood there until they had faded into the night; then he turned and jogged in a wide loop that brought him up on the farmhouse from the rear. Eight or nine men were huddled under an oak tree, each of them so intent on the farmhouse that they didn't hear him glide up.

"—tired of waiting," Travers was complaining. "I say we go in now."

"I don't understand that girl," Bascomb said. "I don't understand her at all. She's nothing like her mother."

"You gave her a chance to come out," the lawman said. "She refused."

"I don't want her hurt, Lloyd."

"I can't guarantee—" Travers began.

The mayor gripped the lawman's shirt. "I mean it. She's not to be harmed. The others, yes, exterminate them."

"Rosemary Utley too?"

"We'll let it out that the farmer and his son resisted arrest and the mother was hit by a stray bullet."

"What about that damn bastard in buckskins?"

"I'd like him alive."

"What for? That might be hard to do."

"Granted. But I'd love to tie him from a rail in the barn and beat on him with a hammer or a rock."

"You and your cruel streak." Marshal Travers laughed. "Why not hang him like you did Lucas?"

"You just said it yourself. I'm as cruel as they come. Now let's get on with it."

16

Fargo didn't have a clear shot at either. He didn't dare try to get closer or he'd be spotted. He stayed flat in the grass as the men levered rounds into their rifles or cocked their revolvers. At a command from Travers they moved toward the back door, the mayor in the middle.

No one showed any interest in the Ovaro, which suited Fargo just fine.

Marshal Travers growled an order and two men rushed the door and hit it with their shoulders. Whooping and yelling, the rest charged inside.

The moment the last man was over the threshold, Fargo was in motion. He raced to the Ovaro, undid the reins, and swung on. He reined around the house, intending to quickly catch up to the Utleys and Joan, but suddenly a figure separated from the darkness. He glimpsed a man holding a rifle by the barrel and sought to shift away from the blow, but his head exploded and he fell into an emptiness as bleak and black as the bottom of a well.

The next sensation Fargo felt was that of swaying. His head hurt like hell and his wrists were in agony. He became aware that his boots weren't touching the ground, and that the pain in his wrists was due to a rope. He opened his eyes and the pain became worse. Inadvertently, he groaned.

"Look who's finally come around."

"Better go tell the marshal and the mayor."

Fargo squinted in the glare of sunlight streaming in the open barn doors. He had been unconscious the whole night.

His mouth felt as if it were filled with cactus. A hand gripped his boots and turned him and he looked down into the sweaty face of Deputy Olsen.

"We meet again, mister."

Fargo licked his dry lips.

"What might your name be, anyhow?"

"I could use some water."

"I bet you could. But we're under orders not to give you a drop. The mayor wants you to suffer a while before he puts you out of your misery."

"You call yourself a lawman?"

"Hey, now. You're the one going around shooting people and bashing heads."

Fargo raised his. The rope around his wrists was so tight, it had broken the flesh and dry blood caked his forearms. The other end of the rope had been thrown over the center beam.

"Nothing to say?" Deputy Olsen said.

"I could still use that water."

Olsen leaned against a stall. "You're as hard as nails. I'll give you that. But it won't help you much when Bascomb gets here."

As coincidence would have it, in barreled the mayor and the deputy who had fetched him, along with the marshal. Bascomb stopped directly under Fargo, reached up, and punched him on the ankle.

"Do I have your attention?"

Fargo glared.

"I do. Good. So let's get to it." Bascomb laced his fingers behind his back. "Where did my daughter get to?"

"She's on her way to Oregon."

"And the Utleys?"

"They went to report you to a federal marshal."

"Liar," Bascomb said. "Double-damned liar. I have men watching the road out of Promise so I know my daughter is still somewhere near. As for the Utleys, federal marshals haven't been given jurisdiction over this territory yet, as you no doubt know."

"He thinks he's clever," Marshal Travers said.

"Someone find something I can hit him with," Mayor Bascomb said.

Olsen and the other deputy began searching.

The mayor put his hands on his pudgy hips. "You've caused me no end of trouble, Buckskin. I'd like to know why."

"Find a mirror."

Bascomb glared. "You do think you're clever, don't you? But you'll tell me what I want or you'll—" He stopped in surprise.

Off to the west shots cracked, three of them, one right after the other.

"The signal," Marshal Travers said. "The men we sent out must have spotted your daughter and the Utleys."

The mayor hustled to the door. "Hang around, clever man," he said sarcastically to Fargo. "After I deal with my darling Joan, I'll be back to deal with you."

Travers beckoned, and Olsen and the other deputy came over. "Stay here and guard the prisoner. You're not to go near him. You're not to give him anything. Is that understood?"

"You can depend on us, Marshal," Olsen said.

"Don't mess up," Travers said, and went out.

Hooves thudded and quiet fell.

"How about that water?" Fargo said.

"I already told you no twice," Olsen replied. "Quit pestering us."

"Some food, then?" Fargo said. "Mrs. Utley made stew. There's plenty left in the pot on the stove."

The other deputy rubbed his stomach. "I sure could use some grub. We haven't eaten since we left town."

"I'm hungry too," Olsen said. "Why don't you go bring bowls for both of us and I'll stand watch?"

Fargo needed both of them to leave. "What do you think will happen to the house if the Utleys are caught?"

Olsen and the other deputy shared puzzled looks. "How the hell would we know? Maybe the mayor will take over their property. Or maybe he'll burn it down."

"That's too bad," Fargo said quietly as if to himself. "I wouldn't mind having that sack of coins. He didn't have time to run up and get it."

"What are you babbling about?"

"Clyde Utley. He's one of those who doesn't trust banks. There's a bunch of coins in a poke up in their bedroom."

"How much are we talking about?" the other deputy asked.

"Not a lot," Fargo said. He knew that deputies in small towns seldom made more than thirty dollars a month. Often it was considerably less. So he said, "No more than a couple of hundred."

"A couple of hundred?" the other deputy repeated, greed writ plain on his face.

"So what?" Deputy Olsen said.

"We could split it two ways."

"Travers would have our hides."

"No one but you and me would know."

Olsen jerked a thumb at Fargo. "He'd know."

"Not if we shoot him before the others get back. We can say he got down somehow and was trying to escape."

"Forget it."

"A hundred dollars each," the other deputy said. "That's

more money than I've had at one time in a month of Sundays."

"Forget it, I said."

"You're courting that gal on Reuben Street, aren't you? Think of all the things you could buy her."

"Goddamn you, Jarrod."

"A hundred dollars," Jarrod stressed. "You can wait here while I go find it."

Deputy Olsen wrestled with himself, and lost. "She has had her eyes on a new dress."

Jarrod laughed and clapped him on the arm. "Now you're talking. I'll be right back." He sped out of the barn as if his boots were on fire.

Fargo hung limp to give the impression he had lost all hope. "He must be a good friend of yours."

Olsen glanced up. "Don't you ever shut up? And no, we work together but we're not pards or anything."

"Ah," Fargo said.

"What the hell does that mean?"

"I'm sure he'll be honest with you and tell you if he finds the poke."

"Why wouldn't he?"

"Two hundred dollars is a lot more than a hundred," Fargo said.

Deputy Olsen glanced at the farmhouse. He began to pace and to mutter. Suddenly he ran off, shouting Jarrod's name.

Fargo didn't waste a second. Bunching his shoulders, he whipped his legs toward his chest. His boots rose level with his face. His stomach taut, he tried again. This time his boots were head high, which still wasn't good enough. Grabbing hold of the rope, he bent his body in half upward. His boots were in front of his nose, and then even with his forehead. His whole body straining, he raised them as high as his hands.

Now came the hard part. He let go of the rope with his right hand and pried at his pant leg. His shoulders were in torment, his left arm a welter of pain. He slid his right hand into his boot and palmed the Arkansas toothpick. Carefully easing it out, he just as carefully reversed his grip, lowered his legs, and cut at the rope. The double-edged blade was as sharp as a straight razor. Strands parted like thin threads. He was almost through when the rope snapped.

Fargo came down hard on his bootheels. Pain shot up his legs into his hips and he nearly toppled. Recovering, he moved to the doorway. The deputies were nowhere around. He ran past the outhouse and the garden. The Ovaro was near the back door, the Henry still in the scabbard. He slid the toothpick into its sheath and yanked the rifle out.

The kitchen was empty. He was halfway across when he saw his revolver on the counter. Someone had left it there when they disarmed him. He twirled it into his holster.

Voices upstairs told him where the pair were. Fargo went up the steps three at a stride. At the top he sidled along the wall until he came to Clyde and Rosemary's bedroom.

". . . should have made him tell us where it's hid." That was Jarrod.

"We never should have listened to him. If the marshal comes back and we're not in the barn—"

"Quit your damn worrying. The poke has to be here somewhere."

"Unless he lied."

"What can he do? He's twenty feet up, hanging from a rope. Look in the closet. I'll tear the bed apart."

Fargo stepped into the doorway with the Henry at his hip. "The Utleys might not like that too much."

Both deputies spun.

"Oh, hell," Olsen said.

112

Jarrod went for his pistol. He had it almost out when the Henry blasted and lead ripped from his sternum to his spine and into the wall behind him.

Olsen flung his hands at the ceiling. "Not me!" he said. "I don't want to die."

"Shuck your hardware."

His throat bobbing, Olsen complied.

"You should be a gambler," Fargo said. "You have more luck than most."

"I do?"

"I'm letting you live."

"You are?"

"Provided you give Mayor Bascomb a message for me."

"*Another* message?"

"Either that or I can shoot you."

"I'm all ears," Deputy Olsen said.

"Tell that walking pastry that so far I've been holding back. But not anymore."

"God help us."

"I want you to let him know where he can find me."

"You do?"

"Yes," Fargo said, and told him.

17

It took over an hour for Fargo to gather the firewood he needed and pile it around Bascomb's country house, as they called it. He picked mostly green wood that would give off a lot of smoke. He also placed small piles of dry grass for kindling.

When he was done, Fargo hid the Ovaro in the trees and went into the stable and up into the hayloft. He opened the loft door and lay on his belly in the straw with the Henry beside him and waited. He could see a good long way to the south, and that was the direction they would come from.

He was going to end it. The mayor and the marshal were corrupt to the core. An accounting was due.

Fargo figured it would be noon when they showed and he wasn't much off the mark. By the sun it was pushing one when dust rose in the distance with stick riders in the thick of the cloud. He hurried down and lit each pile of grass and the grass combusted the tree limbs. Coils of smoke spread along the ground and up the sides of the house.

Returning to the loft, Fargo tucked the Henry to his shoulder and put his cheek to the rifle. The stick riders were larger. The mayor and the marshal were coming on fast. There looked to be twenty men with them. Only a handful were regular deputies. The rest were ordinary townsfolk and maybe some farmers, deputized for the occasion. He would spare them if he could.

Soon smoke covered most of the house in a writhing gray blanket and a sinuous column rose to the sky. Flames licked at the walls. A window shattered and the fire began to devour the inside as well as the outside.

Fargo could see the riders clearly. Mayor Bascomb and Marshal Travers were out in front. Bascomb was a terrible rider; he bounced and flounced, flapping his arms like a goose trying to take wing.

Fargo was hoping they would ride right up to the house. Two swift shots and it would be over. But they drew rein out of rifle range. Bascomb appeared to be giving orders. The riders milled, and among them were two familiar figures, held at gunpoint.

Fargo swore.

Bascomb gave more orders and the whole party advanced. Rosemary sat her saddle straight and proud but Clyde was slumped over and there was a red stain on his shirt from his shoulder wound.

Fargo didn't see Joan or Troy.

Bascomb was grinning. His house was on fire and he was grinning. He came within a few dozen yards of the sheets of flame and drew rein. Rising in the stirrups, he hollered, "Buckskin! I know you can hear me. Olsen gave me your message. Now I have one for you." He motioned, and half a dozen guns were trained on the Utleys.

Fargo centered the Henry's sight on the bastard's chest. All it would take was a stroke of the trigger. But he relaxed his trigger finger.

"Can you guess what it is?" Bascomb gloated. "You have one minute to show yourself or your friends, here, will be shot to pieces."

Several of the men in the posse didn't like that. They said something, objecting. Marshal Travers angrily silenced them.

Bascomb ignored the squabble. He was eagerly scanning the yard and the trees. "I'm not bluffing. I don't care if one of them is a woman. She helped her son take my daughter. She's broken the law, and is no different from any other outlaw."

Fargo wondered if Bascomb really believed that. Men like him often believed their own lies.

"Less than half a minute," the mayor yelled. "You'd better hurry, Buckskin, or they are dead. So help me."

Fargo could barely hear him over the crackling and hissing of the flames and the snap and pop of the burning house. He ran to the ladder and quickly descended. Holding the rifle over his head, he walked from the stable into the sunlight.

The mayor and the marshal and half the posse gigged their mounts.

"I have you now, you son of a bitch," Bascomb crowed as he drew rein. "I can snap my fingers and have you blown to hell."

"But you won't," Fargo said.

"Why not?"

"Because I know where your daughter will be at midnight tonight and I can lead you there."

"It won't wash," Marshal Travers said. "The Utleys say they don't have any idea where the girl and the boy got to."

"Joan and Troy agreed to meet up with me if we were separated," Fargo said. "They wanted my help getting to the Oregon Trail."

"He's lying," Marshal Travers said.

"I'm not so sure," the mayor said.

"You want your daughter back," Fargo told him, "I'll help you on one condition."

"We should just shoot him," Travers said.

"No." Bascomb brought his mount closer. "You're in no position to dictate demands."

"All I want is for you to let Rosemary and her husband go," Fargo said.

"Don't listen to him," Marshal Travers said. "We'll find your daughter anyway. I'll have men comb the entire countryside."

"It's a lot of territory," Bascomb said, his brow puckered.

"Do we have a deal?" Fargo asked.

"I'm thinking," Bascomb said.

"Damn it, Harry," Marshal Travers growled. "He's playing us for fools."

"I want Joan back more than anything."

"Oh, hell."

Bascomb reached under his jacket and drew out a pocket pistol. He cocked it and pointed it at Fargo's legs. "I could make you tell me."

"Maybe you could and maybe you couldn't," Fargo said with a calmness he didn't feel. "Or maybe I'd bleed to death and couldn't tell you if I wanted."

"Shoot him," the marshal urged.

"Be quiet, Lloyd," Bascomb said. "You're distracting me and I need a clear head."

"Spare the Utleys," Fargo said. "What harm can it do?"

"Not the son," Bascomb said. "He must pay."

"I didn't ask you to spare him."

"No, you didn't." Bascomb slid the pocket pistol back under his jacket.

"Damn, damn, damn," Marshal Travers said.

"All right, you have your deal," Mayor Bascomb said, and bent forward. "But understand something. If you're lying to me, if this is another of your tricks, you'll die the most horrible death you can imagine."

"I'm not stupid," Fargo said.

"No, you're almost as shrewd as me. That's a compliment I rarely give. Most people are as dumb as oxen."

"Thanks a lot," Marshal Travers said.

"I didn't say you, Lloyd," the mayor said. "Quit your damn bellyaching and have a deputy relieve our friend here of his hardware." He paused. "What *is* your name, by the way?"

"Kit Carson."

"Be serious."

"Daniel Boone."

"Fine. Keep it to yourself. You won't merit a tombstone anyway."

Marshal Travers raised an arm and motioned and the Utleys were brought up. Rosemary wearily smiled at Fargo. Clyde nodded.

"You are free to go," Mayor Bascomb informed them.

"What have you done?" Rosemary asked.

"He's struck a deal to have you spared," Bascomb said. "I'd take advantage, were I you, and leave before I change my mind."

"We can go home?" Clyde said.

"I didn't say that. I want you gone. Out of my sight and out of Promise and out of this country."

"But our farm," Clyde said. "All our belongings."

"You just sold your farm to me." Bascomb reached into a pocket and produced a coin. "For a silver dollar. I, in turn, will sell it to the next homesteaders who come along for all I can get for it."

"That's robbery," Clyde said.

"It's justice," Bascomb said, "for your part in the kidnapping of my daughter." He raised a hand when Clyde went to speak. "Give me any more guff and the deal is off. I'll have you thrown in jail and you can take your chance in court."

"That's no chance at all," Rosemary said. "You'll rig the trial so we're convicted."

"At least one of you has brains," Bascomb said.

"Where will we go?" Clyde said. "What will we do?"

"That's your problem," Bascomb was looking at Rosemary. "What will it be?"

"You win," she said.

"Of course I do," Bascomb crowed. "I always win." He reined his horse close to hers and gave her the coin. "So it's good and legal."

"You're a despicable human being."

"Now, now. Don't make me mad." Bascomb turned to the marshal. "Have a deputy escort them three or four miles north of town."

"You never take my advice," Travers said.

Bascomb sighed and closed his eyes and pinched the bridge of his nose. "I swear, you are giving me a headache. When will you get it through your head that this is about my daughter and nothing else?"

Rosemary hadn't taken her eyes off Fargo. "Thank you for trying."

"Less than twelve hours and it will be over," Fargo said.

"Get them out of here," the mayor ordered.

"Can we stop in Promise and have the doctor look at my husband?" Rosemary asked.

"No."

Marshal Travers had Deputy Olsen usher the Utleys away.

"Good riddance," Mayor Bascomb said.

The marshal climbed down and personally relieved Fargo of the Henry and the Colt. "Were it up to me you wouldn't be breathing."

"Were it up to me neither would you."

Travers made as if to hit him with the Colt but glanced at

the mayor and lowered his arm. "Once he has his daughter, you're worm food."

"I hear you were a lawman down in Texas," Fargo said.

Travers acted surprised that he'd brought it up. "So?"

"Were you as rotten at it down there as you are here?"

"I run a decent town," Travers snapped. "Anyone can walk the street at any time of the day or night without fear for their life."

"So long as you and the mayor aren't mad at them," Fargo said.

Wheeling, Travers stalked off.

Roaring flames engulfed the house and a giant column of smoke had to be visible for miles. Suddenly, with a tremendous crash, a side wall collapsed, causing several of the horses to shy. A glittering shower of sparks rose into the sky like a legion of fireflies.

Mayor Bascomb watched them, then turned and smiled coldly at Fargo. "Another thing I owe you for. And mark my words. You're going to pay."

18

Fargo pondered as they rode. It was ironic that Bascomb's love for his daughter was keeping him alive. At midnight, though, Bascomb would realize what Travers already suspected, namely, that he hadn't arranged to meet up with Joan and Troy. He had bought his life with a lie. Now all he had to do was think of a way to escape.

It helped that the posse had shrunk. With the Utleys on their way to Oregon, and him in custody, Travers had sent all but eight men home. The mayor grumbled about it, saying they should call out the whole town until Joan was back where she belonged.

Now here they were, heading west toward the foothills, Fargo surrounded by nervous deputies with their hands on their revolvers.

Marshal Travers brought his mount alongside the Ovaro.

"Harry is smart as hell but he can be stupid."

"There's a lot of that going around," Fargo said.

"That girl of his is his blind spot. His— What do folks call it? Achilles' heel?"

"I figured it was pies and pastries."

Travers laughed. "He does have a belly, doesn't he? But it's not him I want to talk about."

"What then?"

"I'm real curious about who you are. You refuse to say,

and you don't have anything on you or in your saddlebags that gives us a clue."

"I'm the Man With No Name," Fargo said.

"You're somebody," Travers said. "Not just an ordinary somebody, either. You can shoot. You can fight. You track."

"A lot of men can."

"Not as good as you." Travers shook his head. "No, you're somebody special. It hit me when you said you were Kit Carson that you're a lot like him. It got me to thinking."

"I'm surprised you know how."

"Someone with your talents makes me think that maybe you make your living as a scout."

"Or it could be I'm a store clerk."

Travers shook his head. "No, you're a scout, all right. There aren't that many of your kind around and most of those there are work for the army." The marshal looked at him. "How about you? You ever worked for the army?"

"Those gents who like to wear uniforms and blow on bugles?"

"I've been asking myself, who have I ever heard of that fits a man like you? There's Carson but he's as short as the mayor and you're as tall as me. There's Jim Bridger, but he's getting on in years. O'Grady got himself killed and scalped by the Blackfeet last year."

"There are a lot more."

"But not many as quick as you. Olsen told me he's never seen anyone so fast on the draw. Hell, he's never even *heard* of anyone as fast." Travers paused. "Except for one man."

"Oh?"

"This man's a tough son of a bitch. He's got a nickname, you might call it. Just as folks call Zebulon Pike the Path-finder, they have a name for this scout I'm thinking of. They call him the Trailsman."

"Never heard of him," Fargo said.

"They say he's been everywhere. He's lived with the Apaches and the Sioux. He's been in shooting contests that were written up in the newspapers. He's even been in the penny dreadfuls. I guess you could say he's famous."

"Middling famous, maybe," Fargo said.

"This gent has a peculiar name, which is why it's easy to remember," Travers paused. "His name is Skye Fargo."

"You're right. It is peculiar."

"I think you're him."

"Be hard to prove."

"Don't need to," the lawman said. "By this time tomorrow you'll be dead and it won't hardly matter."

"Then why bring it up?"

"I want you to know I'm not as dumb as you seem to think I am," Travers said. "Maybe I'm not the most upstanding law dog who ever lived—"

"No maybe about it," Fargo said.

"—but I'm not stupid. So are you him or aren't you?"

"Who?"

Travers smiled a cold smile. "Didn't really expect you to admit it." He used his spurs and caught up to the mayor.

Fargo didn't care that the lawman had guessed. It couldn't help him in any way.

The deputy on Fargo's right—Simmons, the one who had been at the jail when Fargo broke Troy out—brought his sorrel in close. "I heard what the marshal and you were talking about."

"Good for you."

"Are you really him? Fargo, I mean."

"Does it make a difference?"

"It sure as hell does, even if the marshal can't see it." Simmons glanced at Travers's back. "We kill somebody like you, others might come snooping around, wondering where you got to."

Fargo latched on to the notion and went with it. "I hadn't thought of that but you're right. Colonel Webster will likely send a patrol out."

"Who?"

Fargo was beginning to lose count of his fibs. "He's in charge at Fort Laramie. I'm under orders to report to him and was on my way there when I stopped in Promise." In fact, he wasn't working for the army at the moment, and was entirely on his own.

"The hell you say."

"Or maybe the colonel will come himself and keep looking until he finds out what happened to me."

"Hell, hell, hell," Simmons said.

"The army doesn't hang murderers, though," Fargo mentioned as if that was a good thing.

"They don't?"

"No. They throw them in a stockade for the rest of their lives."

Simmons looked worried. "I don't like this. I don't like it one little bit. No one ever said anything about tangling with the army." He reined away and spent the next half an hour chewing on his lower lip.

Fargo smothered a grin. He'd planted a seed that might take root.

For the next hour they pushed on. Then, midway up a mile-long grade that climbed to the hills, Marshal Travers called a halt.

The mayor didn't like it. "What are we stopping for? The sooner we get to where he's to meet her, the sooner my daughter will be back where she belongs."

"The horses need rest," Travers said. "Unless you'd rather ride them into the ground."

That shut the mayor up.

Fargo squatted and plucked at the grass. He noticed Simmons and several others huddled together. Only one deputy was standing guard over him, and the man kept glancing at his huddled friends as if he was anxious to join them. Suddenly the man stiffened.

A shadow fell over Fargo and Marshal Travers came around in front of him. "Ready to admit who you are?"

"Ready to arrest Bascomb and turn yourself in?" Fargo rejoined.

"You never give up," Travers said. "But if you think I'll have a twinge of conscience, think again."

Fargo had figured as much. "Is there anything you won't do? How are you at kicking babies?"

Travers balled his fists. "Say what you will. The folks in Promise sleep in peace at night, thanks to me."

"Except for the innocent man you helped hang."

"You don't know when to quit," Travers said. "Keep this up and you'll suffer that much more."

"I bet you *would* kick a baby," Fargo said.

Travers glowered and moved off and his shadow was replaced by a shorter one.

"What were you two talking about?" Mayor Bascomb asked. "Lloyd seems mad."

"He didn't like it when I told him that he does all the work and you get most of the money," Fargo replied, and almost chuckled. He was getting good at this.

Bascomb gave a slight start. "Why did you bring a thing like that up?"

"He mentioned the Utleys. You plan to take over their

farm and sell it. I wondered how much of the money you'd keep and how much would go to Travers."

"I've always been generous with Lloyd," Bascomb said. "He gets ten percent of most everything."

"Ten whole percent."

The mayor's round cheeks puffed out. "I am growing to detest you. You have been nothing but a thorn in my side from the moment you rode into town."

"I didn't take your horse," Fargo said. "Your trained coyote took mine."

"Is that what this has been about? You're upset that we impounded your animal and levied a fine?"

"Mainly this is about you being a bastard."

Bascomb swore. "All I can say is that my daughter'd better be where you say she will or you will rue the day you were born."

"I haven't rued in a coon's age," Fargo said.

The mayor stalked off.

Fargo sat back and rested his arms on his knees. He had the whole pack of them stirred up. Now all he could do was wait and see if he'd benefit.

After ten minutes the marshal barked for them to mount. Once again Fargo was ringed by deputies. Simmons was one, and they hadn't gone a hundred yards when he reined in close.

"Got a question for you."

"Monongahela," Fargo said.

"What?"

"You were about to ask my favorite whiskey. I'm partial to Monongahela."

"No. I was about to ask about the army sending a patrol out to find you."

"I said they might."

"How would they know to nose around Promise?"

"I told the colonel I was coming this way," Fargo added to his mountain of untruths. "And there aren't any other settlements along this stretch of the Oregon Trail."

"No," Simmons had to admit. "There aren't." He muttered something and then said, "That does it."

"Does what?"

"Nothing." Simmons fell back and began talking to two others.

This time Fargo didn't smother his smile.

19

A sliver of golden arch was all that remained of the setting sun. Already a few stars sparkled.

Fargo gazed about them. He had deliberately brought the posse into the hills; here there were forest and bluffs and washes, plenty of cover for a man who might have hard riding to do.

After spending most of the day in the saddle, the deputies weren't as alert as they should have been. They were tired and uneasy, thanks to his little lie about the army.

The mayor and the marshal were up ahead. All afternoon they had bickered. They didn't do it loud enough for anyone to overhear but Fargo had a hunch what they were arguing about. Another seed had sprouted.

As night unfolded its black blanket, Marshal Travers called another halt. No sooner did Fargo climb down and stretch than Mayor Bascomb barreled up to him and poked him in the chest.

"I should have you shot."

"You do and you'll never see your daughter again," Fargo said.

"Lloyd has pestered me all afternoon about how he should have a bigger share in things."

"He's getting as greedy as you."

"Greed, hell," Bascomb spat. "I don't care about money.

It's a means to what I really care about." He swelled out his chest. "To power."

"You sure do like to lord it over folks," Fargo conceded.

"I do it for their own good. Most people are sheep. They blunder through life with no set purpose." Bascomb raised his chin as if posing for a portrait. "Not me. I never do anything without a reason. My whole life is devoted to one end and one end alone."

"Power," Fargo said.

"You say it like it's a dirty word. But you saw Promise. It's the perfect community. And it's my doing."

"I got the impression the marshal thought it was his."

"He's nothing without me."

"The great and mighty Harry Bascomb."

"Look down your nose at me if you must but I have no regrets. If I had everything to do over again, I'd do it exactly the same."

"That include hanging the farmer?"

Bascomb turned on a heel and left him.

A deputy went up to Marshal Travers and asked if it would be all right to kindle a fire for coffee. Travers said no. They had hours of riding yet. Coffee, and supper, must wait. The deputies did more huddling, and grumbled. No one paid any attention to Fargo.

The Ovaro was a few feet away, the reins dangling. As casually as he could, Fargo took hold of them and stepped in close to the saddle. No one noticed.

Nearby stood the marshal's mount. Fargo knew that his Colt was in Travers's saddlebags, and that the marshal had stuck the Henry in his bedroll.

Fargo hiked a leg, and froze. Simmons had turned in his direction. He thought for sure the deputy would holler to warn the others but Simmons turned back again. Fargo slid his boot into the stirrup, gripped the saddle horn, and was in the saddle and reining around before anyone could collect their wits. A jab of his spurs and he was next to the marshal's animal and snagged its reins. Shouts broke out and a shot banged but by then he was galloping into the night.

"After him!" Mayor Bascomb bellowed. "Don't let him get away!"

Fargo reached a tract of woods and drew rein. Vaulting down, he opened Travers's saddlebags and rummaged inside. His fingers closed on the Colt. Jamming his other hand into the bedroll, he grabbed the Henry by the barrel and pulled.

Hooves thudded and men yelled as Fargo sprang to the Ovaro, shoved the Henry into the scabbard, and was on and away before the first of his pursuers crashed into the timber.

To discourage them, Fargo twisted and fired twice.

"He has a gun!" someone bawled.

Pistols cracked. Lead buzzed and whined and clipped a branch near Fargo's head. He didn't shoot back. The important thing was to put distance between them.

Bascomb was hollering up a storm. Something about five hundred dollars for the man who caught him.

Not again, Fargo vowed. Twice he'd been taken prisoner and disarmed. There wouldn't be a third time.

For a quarter of an hour Fargo rode like a Chinook wind. When at last he drew rein and cocked his head to listen, the only sounds were those of the wild: coyotes and wolves and the screech of a hunting owl.

Fargo relaxed for the first time all day. He was free and in his element. He could go anywhere. But where? he asked himself. Into town wouldn't be smart. By now everyone must have heard about the "man in buckskins" who was causing so much trouble. He could try to overtake Rosemary and

Clyde but they had a day's head start and the Ovaro was tired.

The thing to do, he told himself, was to take the fight to Bascomb and Travers. He'd burned the mayor's country house down but that had been to lure them into his rifle sights. Now he needed to go after *them*.

He decided that what he needed most was to rest up for a couple of days and then wage his war anew. But where to rest?

An idea blossomed, and Fargo chuckled. It was the last place they'd expect him to go.

Reining around, he struck off cross-country and rode long into the night. Dawn was less than an hour off when he came to a weary stop at the rear of the Utley farmhouse.

No one was there. With Rosemary and Clyde gone, and Troy and Joan on the run, Marshal Travers had taken all his deputies away.

Fargo climbed down. He led the stallion around the house and into the barn and put it in a stall. He stripped off the saddle and saddle blanket and took off the bridle. He found oats in a bin and a pitchfork for the hay.

His rifle in the bend of his elbow, Fargo returned to the house. He lit a lamp in the kitchen and placed it on the floor with the wick low so the window wouldn't be brightly lit. Ravenous, he helped himself to the pantry's bounty: a thick slab of salted beef, green beans, onions and carrots and potatoes. He got the stove hot and soon the delicious aroma of cooking food filled the kitchen.

His stomach wouldn't stop growling. Fargo chewed on a raw carrot but it didn't help. He made coffee, strong and black, and when he set down to the table he had a feast spread before him.

Fargo went heavy on the salt. He didn't use a lot on the

trail, so when he could treat himself, he did. He smeared butter on the bread and crammed half a slice into his mouth at a bite. The potatoes melted in his mouth. He liked to spear a green bean and a carrot with each forkful and mix the taste. The coffee about burned his throat. He was on his second helping of everything and reaching for the loaf of bread when a tingle ran down his spine. From somewhere in the farmhouse came a light thump.

Instantly Fargo was on his feet with the Colt in his hand. Advancing to the hall, he stopped. The house was quiet but he was sure he had heard it. He checked the parlor and the other downstairs rooms without finding anything or anyone.

He crept to the foot of the stairs—just as, up above, there was another thump.

Fargo climbed on the balls of his feet. The upstairs hall was empty. The door to Rosemary and Clyde's bedroom was open but the door to Troy's was closed.

Fargo kept his back to the wall. His hand was on the latch when a third thump confirmed what he's suspected—someone was in Troy's bedroom. "Oh, hell," he said, and called out, "Joan? Troy? Is that you?"

Someone whispered and the door was jerked open and Joan impulsively flew at him and hugged him.

"Thank God it's you! We were so scared."

"I wasn't," Troy said sullenly. His face wasn't as swollen but he still looked terrible.

"What are you doing here?" Fargo asked. "I thought you got away safe."

"We did," Joan said. "But I have unfinished business with my father. So we circled back and just got here a while ago. Our horses are in the apple orchard."

Fargo recollected seeing four or five apples trees out back of the barn.

"Where are my ma and pa?" Troy asked. "We got separated and I was worried the mayor got his hands on them."

"He did," Fargo said, and related how he had bargained for their lives. "So far as I know," he concluded, "they're on their way to Oregon."

"Some help you are."

"Troy!" Joan said.

"Well, he hasn't been much, has he? We need my parents. We can't do this ourselves."

"I'll help you," Fargo said.

Troy snorted.

"Troy Adam Utley, you stop that this instant," Joan said. "He's nearly been killed for our sake. He deserves your respect."

"If you say so."

"Any ideas on how to turn the tables on my father?" Joan asked Fargo.

"There's only one way to end it that I can see," Fargo said.

Joan nodded. "I should have done it years ago."

"You're a girl."

"So?"

"So girls don't do what you have in mind."

"But boys do?"

"No one should have to," Fargo said, wondering why she was becoming so bothered about it.

"Let me be perfectly clear," Joan said. "My father doesn't deserve to live."

Before Fargo could reply, thunder that wasn't thunder resounded out of the depths of the night.

Joan grasped his wrist in alarm. "Someone's coming."

"Maybe it's the marshal," Troy said.

Fargo doubted it. "Stay here," he said, and raced downstairs and out the front door. A patch of dark shadow rendered him next to invisible.

The riders were almost there. As best Fargo could judge, there were only two or three. Pressing the Henry to his shoulder, he took aim at an oncoming figure. He started to thumb back the hammer. "I'll be damned," he said, and lowered the rifle.

The night disgorged the last people Fargo expected to see.

Rosemary and Clyde came to a stop and she reached over to steady him. Clyde was doubled over and clinging to his saddle with what little strength he had left.

"We'll get you inside and I'll put a fresh bandage on," Rosemary said. "Then you're to stay in bed for a day."

"Can't," Clyde said. "They'll be after us."

"This is our home," Rosemary said. "No one is running us off. Not the marshal. Not that awful Mayor Bascomb. Not anyone."

"Good to hear," Fargo said, stepping out where they could see him.

Rosemary squealed in delight and climbed down and gave him a warm hug. "It's so good to see you. I thought they would have killed you by now."

"They've been trying."

Fargo helped Clyde down and supported him while Rosemary opened the front door and stood aside for them to enter.

"Take him upstairs. I need to get food into him."

Joan and Troy came running down and Rosemary enfolded her son in his arms.

"This is glorious. My family is back together."

Clyde was in a bad way. He had lost a lot of blood and was in and out of consciousness. Fargo eased him onto their bed and sat on the edge.

"Didn't expect to see you again so soon."

Clyde's eyelids fluttered and he licked his lips. "Her doing," he said. "She told Deputy Olsen her cinch was loose and he let her stop to tighten it." Clyde managed a chuckle. "She hit him over the head with a rock when his back was turned. She has spunk, my gal."

"You've been riding ever since?"

Clyde nodded and said weakly, "Took forever to get here. Wasn't good for my shoulder." With that he passed out.

Fargo would have left but Rosemary bustled in and enlisted his aid in taking off Clyde's shirt. The old bandage was more red than white, and Clyde's shoulder and back and upper arm were covered with dry blood.

"Please don't let him die," Rosemary said to the ceiling. She placed her hand on her husband's chest. "You should have seen him. He didn't complain once the whole time."

"He's a tough old bird."

"Oh, it wasn't that," Rosemary said, affectionately caressing Clyde's brow. "He knew how much I wanted to come back and knew I'd make him stop if he told me about the bleeding."

"I hear you beaned Olsen with a rock?"

Rosemary smiled. "Hard as I could. I'm sorry to say he was alive when we left. I heard him groan."

"They'll be coming, then."

"I'm afraid so."

20

"We're right back where we started," Rosemary Utley remarked.

Fargo hadn't thought of that, but they were. With a difference. This time he'd have a little surprise for Bascomb and Travers.

"I couldn't do it," Rosemary was saying. "I couldn't give up our farm, our home, our life. No one has the right to force people to do that."

"No," Fargo agreed.

"I made up my mind we were coming back and tricked Deputy Olsen and here we are. But I don't know what to do next." Rosemary wearily sagged. "I am open to ideas."

"I'll take care of that end of it."

"I'm glad you're here," Rosemary said. "If you weren't I'm afraid they would overpower us and either make us leave again or put us on trial."

"Or do you in," Fargo said.

"Do you really think they would? Kill innocent people?"

"They killed Lucas. They killed him legally but they killed him."

"The world can be a terrible place."

"It's not the world so much," Fargo said, thinking of the majesty of the mountains on a bright summer's day and the rolling green of prairie grass rippling in the breeze. "It's the people."

"Yes," Rosemary said. "The Bascombs and the Traverses of the world."

"There will be two less of them before this is done."

Rosemary raised her sorrowful eyes to his. "I wouldn't want you to do it on our account."

"I'm not."

"You're a good man," Rosemary said.

"Depends on your notion of good," Fargo said. By some standards, his fondness for females, whiskey and cards would brand him as evil.

Rosemary washed and bandaged her husband and prepared breakfast.

Fargo hadn't eaten that long ago but he ate again. He wolfed his eggs and bacon and took his time with his coffee.

"When do you reckon they will show?" Troy asked at one point.

Fargo had been calculating the miles and the time it would take for Olsen to return to Promise and for Marshal Travers to organize a new posse. "We can expect them along about sunset or shortly after." He hoped it was after.

"What do you suggest we do until then?" Rosemary asked.

"We'll all get some sleep until one or two," Fargo proposed. "Then I can use your help."

"With what?"

"We need to end this once and for all."

"And you think you have a way? Count me in," Rosemary said. "I owe them for Clyde."

"Count me in, too," Troy said.

Fargo looked at Joan.

"Make it unanimous. And before you say anything about

him being my father, do what you have to. Because if you don't get to him, I will."

"Oh, Joan," Rosemary said.

"I can't pretend I love him when I don't. My whole life since my mother died, he's treated me more like a nuisance than a daughter." Joan reached across the table and put her hand on Fargo's arm. "Don't hold back because of me."

"From now on," Fargo said, "I'm not holding back at all."

They were ready an hour before nightfall. Fargo carried Clyde into the root cellar. Rosemary balked, saying the bed was best, until he pointed out that stray slugs were more likely to pose a danger in the bedroom.

Troy was eager to help fight and mad when Fargo told him to stay with his parents and Joan.

"You can't do it alone. And I'm not a bad shot. Ask my ma."

"I only have the two guns," Fargo said, patting his Colt and wagging his rifle.

"Lend me one and you use the other."

"No, and that's final." Fargo sought to lessen the sting by adding, "One of us has to stay alive to help your folks." He handed down a lamp and shut the trapdoor.

Now all Fargo could do was wait. He went upstairs to a window that faced in the direction of Promise and pulled up a chair. He was rested and refreshed and as ready as he was going to be. The only question was how many would come. Half the town or a handful?

The sun had been down about an hour and a half when the sound he had been waiting for heralded their coming. He ran downstairs and opened the front door and then the back door each about a handbreadth. Close by each door were a box of Lucifers and the empty lamps he had drained of whale oil.

Fargo ran back upstairs and opened the bedroom window. From there he could pinpoint direction better. He expected some of the riders would approach the front of the house while others came at it from the rear but they all came straight on toward the front. He fairly flew down to the front door and was in a crouch with the Lucifers in his hand when the posse slowed.

Fargo struck the first match. The Lucifer crackled and he lowered it to the line of whale oil he had poured. Smoke puffed and flames leaped and raced from the house to the pile of firewood he and the others had spent hours gathering. Larger flames gouted.

There were ten of them. Marshal Travers was in the lead, and at the burst of light he bellowed for his posse to open fire.

Fargo snatched up the Henry and aimed at Travers but just as he fired another rider came between them and the other man pitched from the saddle. Lead smacked the house and a window shattered. Fargo worked the lever, fired, worked the lever, fired again.

Three were down and the rest broke to either side and headed for the back of the house.

Whirling, Fargo raced down the hall to the back door. Again he struck a Lucifer. Again flames shot from the house to the second pile of firewood.

A posse member was dismounting and was caught flat-footed in the glare. He spun and blasted three shots from the hip with a revolver.

Fargo responded once with the Henry. He winged another man unlimbering a Winchester. He sent the hat of a third flying.

Off in the dark Travers shouted and the posse bolted from the ring of firelight.

A hand fell on Fargo's shoulder. Spinning, he nearly bashed the Henry's stock against Troy Utley's head. "What the hell are you doing? You're supposed to be in the root cellar."

"I'm a grown man and this is our home," Troy said. "I have a right to defend it."

Fargo was mad at not being obeyed but now wasn't the time to bring it up. He shoved the Henry into the boy's hands. "Keep watch out front. I'll stay here."

Troy grinned and ran his hand over the brass receiver. "This is the shiniest rifle I ever saw."

"Tell it to the men out there who came to kill you."

"Oh." Troy dashed away.

Fargo drew his Colt. The woodpile was burning nicely and would last a while. For the time being the posse had been thwarted. He took off his hat and placed it aside so he could peer out without being noticed. Someone moved just beyond the firelight.

"That you in there, scout?" Marshal Travers yelled.

"Who else?" Fargo said.

"We were after the old couple," Travers said. "Didn't count on you being here."

"Your mistake."

"I'm making a lot of them lately," Travers said. "You've done shot my posse to pieces."

"I almost had you, too."

The lawman didn't respond right away. When he did, he posed a question. "What would it take to get you to ride off and leave us be?"

"This your idea or the mayor's?"

"He'd throw a fit if he knew I asked. But you're more trouble than most ten hombres. I'd like to be shed of you while we still can. What would it take? Money? I'll give you five hundred dollars to light a shuck."

"Getting nervous, are you?"

"A thousand dollars."

"Not going to happen," Fargo said.

"You aim to see this through?"

"I sure as hell do," Fargo said.

Not long after, hoofbeats drummed.

Troy came from the front room and excitedly squatted next to him. "Didn't you hear them leave?"

"I did," Fargo said.

"Then let's get Joan and her folks out of the root cellar."

"Did you *see* them leave?"

"No. How could I? It's dark as sin out except for the fires."

"Could be not all of them left," Fargo said. "Could be they want us to think they did so whoever didn't go can sneak close and put lead into us."

"I hadn't thought of that," Troy said.

"Stay at the front door until I say different."

The next hour was uneventful. Fargo let another go by before he rose and closed the back door and went to the front to find Troy dozing. He kicked the boy's legs and Troy jumped and almost dropped the Henry. "You fell asleep."

"I did not."

"I just saw you." Fargo bent and relieved him of the rifle.

"I was resting my eyes, is all."

"You don't look eighty years old," Fargo said, and slammed the front door. "Fetch your folks and Joan." He returned to the kitchen and put a fresh batch of coffee on.

When the Utleys and the girl came out of the pantry, Rosemary excused herself and her husband, saying they both needed rest. Joan said she would like a cup and sat at the table. Troy hesitated, then sat next to her.

"You saved us again," Joan said.

"And my hide as well," Fargo pointed out as he opened a cupboard and took down cups and saucers.

"What next? Do we wait for the marshal to come back with a bigger posse?"

"Only if we're stupid," Fargo said.

"I did some thinking while we were down in the root cellar," Joan said, "and I had a brainstorm."

"I'm listening."

"What if I wrote my father a note asking him to come out to the farm alone? I'll tell him I've had a change of heart and I'd like to talk."

"You think he'll buy that?"

"Why wouldn't he, as much as he cares for me? Once he shows up, you can kill him."

Fargo looked at her.

"That's the best solution. So long as he's alive none of us will have a moment's peace."

"Your own father."

"You keep forgetting how much I hate him."

"He's still your father."

"Now you sound like Rosemary." Joan smacked the table in irritation. "Why can't anyone accept that I want to put an end to him and to our troubles?"

"You're forgetting Marshal Travers."

"I'll ask my father to bring Travers along. We'll kill both."

"God, you're bloodthirsty," Troy said.

Joan Bascomb grinned. "You have yet to see the real me."

21

Fargo leaned against the counter. He was mildly troubled by some of her remarks. Hating someone was one thing. Her hate for her father was the kind that ate at a person until the hate took over their whole life. He mentioned as much.

Joan puckered her lips in annoyance. "You're a fine one to talk. You're out to destroy my father and the marshal or die trying."

"It's not the same," Fargo said.

"The hell it isn't. I want a new life with Troy. My father is trying to prevent that. I won't let him. I'll kill him if I have to, and that's that."

"Bucked a lot of people out in gore, have you?" Fargo tried to lighten her mood.

"Tell you what," Joan said. "Give me your solemn word here and now that you'll kill him for me and I'll let it drop."

"I will stop him," Fargo said, "but in my own way and in my own time."

"When? Today? Next week? Next month?"

"I can't predict," Fargo said.

Joan stood and motioned at Troy. "Come on. It's plain we can't count on this scout."

"Aren't you being a little hard on him?" Troy said.

Angrily marching to the hall, Joan looked back. "Him or me. Make up your mind, Troy Utley."

"You. Always you," Troy said, and hurried at her heels like a puppy at its master's.

Fargo sighed. This was the thanks he got for saving them. He supposed he should have been mad but he was too damn tired. He shifted a chair so it faced the back door and sat at the table to wait for the coffee to get done. It promised to be another long night.

He was on his second cup when a gust of wind fanned his face. The back door, though, was still shut. He glanced at the window. It was closed. Curiosity brought him to his feet as another gust cooled his cheeks. He put down his cup and ran down the hall.

"Damn it."

The front door was open.

Fargo went out. A few embers were all that was left of the bonfire. He had to be sure so he went upstairs. Rosemary and Clyde were sawing logs in their bed. Troy's room was empty. His bed hadn't been slept in.

Fargo returned to the parents. He gently shook Rosemary until she mumbled and opened her eyes. Panic filled them, and he put a finger over her mouth to stifle an outcry. "It's all right. The posse hasn't come back. But someone else has gone missing."

Rosemary blinked and rose onto her elbows. "Troy and Joan?"

"Where they got to is anyone's guess but she was talking about killing her father."

"Oh Lord," Rosemary said. "Or she'll have our son do it for her. She has him wrapped around her little finger. And Troy will be the one the law hunts down, not her."

"They don't have much of a head start," Fargo mentioned. "If I leave right away—"

"Do you think you can stop them?" Rosemary sat up. "What

are you waiting for? Clyde and I will be all right. Save our son from making a mistake that could get him hung."

"I'll do what I can," Fargo said.

The Ovaro had rested all day so Fargo could push hard.

He was sure Joan and Troy were heading for town. With the country house burned down, that was where they would find her father. He held to a trot in the hope he would soon overtake them. When it became obvious he wouldn't, he slowed.

Fargo didn't know what Joan was thinking. After all this while, to suddenly want her father dead at all costs made no sense. Or was it sudden? he wondered. Maybe she'd wanted him dead all along and was just tired of waiting for it to get done.

When he saw a campfire he slowed even more. Well out of earshot he dismounted, removed his spurs, and shucked the Henry.

Like a two-legged cat he glided toward it.

There were five of them. Three were wounded and flat on their backs. One wouldn't stop groaning. A coffeepot had been put on but only a couple were drinking. They all looked as miserable as human beings could look. When Fargo strode into the firelight, they froze in fear. None clawed for their hardware.

A man with a tin cup in his hand was the first to recover from the shock. "Damn it, mister. Weren't you satisfied with shooting us to ribbons? You had to come after us to finish us off?"

"Don't go for your guns and I won't," Fargo said.

"We're leaving and don't want any part of you," declared another.

"Where's the marshal?"

"The coldhearted bastard went on without us," said the man with the cup. He gestured at the wounded. "We wouldn't desert our friends but he did."

"I am through with him and I am through with the mayor," said a third man almost savagely.

"How many guns will back them in Promise?" Fargo asked.

The man with the cup shrugged. "Olsen and maybe a few others."

"Simmons?" Fargo said.

The man laughed a bitter laugh. "Hell, he lit out not long after you got away the other night. Took several men with him. Said they didn't want any part of it, that going against you would bring the army down on our heads."

"You are plumb poison," said a wounded man.

Fargo's ruse had worked. He had whittled the odds without having to fire a shot. "You should have gone with them."

"Travers is the law. We were deputized."

"When the law is broken by the men wearing the badges, there is no law. You weren't a posse. You were a pack of killers."

"We were only doing what we were told."

"Your mistake."

"Christ, mister," said the man who had been groaning. "You don't need to rub our noses in it."

"Stay out of this from here on," Fargo warned. "I won't go easy on you."

"What the hell do you call what you did to us at the Utley place? That was some trick with those fires."

Fargo began to back away but stopped. "Have you seen anyone else? The mayor's daughter, maybe?"

"We heard a couple of horses off a ways a while ago but they didn't come close enough for us to see who it was."

Fargo was about to step into the darkness when the groaner brought him up short with an off-handed comment.

"So she's finally going to do it, is she?"

"Do what?" Fargo asked.

"Kill her pa. What else? She's been saying as how she wanted to the whole time they've been in Promise."

"That long?" Fargo said.

Tin cup answered, "Joan Bascomb hates her pa more than anything. Hardly a day went by they didn't have a squabble right out in public. It got so bad, some of the wives got together and went to the mayor and told him something had to be done about how she behaved."

"What did the mayor say?"

"Told them they were busybodies and to mind their own damn business."

"Why does she want him dead so much?" Fargo probed. "He so strict she can't stand it?"

"Something to do with her ma dying when she was little," tin cup said. "She blames him."

"I thought her mother died from consumption."

"To hear the girl talk," tin cup said, "you'd think the mayor poisoned her."

"Son of a bitch," Fargo said.

"To be honest, mister," another remarked, "when she took up with the Utley boy it surprised me. She's always been sort of snooty."

Tin cup nodded. "She was always looking down her nose at anyone who didn't have as much money as they do."

"Which is everybody in Promise," a man said.

Tin cup had more. "The marshal told some of us that she tried to kill her pa not long ago. It's why the mayor took to having the doctor jab a needle into her and tame her down."

Fargo had heard enough. He ran to the Ovaro and fanned the breeze.

The glare of the midmorning sun was hard on Fargo's eyes. From a distance Promise appeared normal. People were moving about in the street. Kids ran and played. Horses were tied to hitch rails. A dog scratched itself. Fargo squinted but saw no trace of Joan Bascomb or Troy Utley.

Fargo circled until he was several hundred yards from the house that Marshal Travers had brought Joan to. To go on in broad daylight invited trouble. Travers would shoot him on sight.

Two furtive forms appeared. They were slinking between houses. They jumped a fence, scooted to the back door, and slipped inside.

Fargo charged at a gallop. He was off the Ovaro while the stallion was in motion and vaulted the fence. At the door he drew his Colt. He put an ear to the wood and cautiously cracked it open. A long hall ran the length of the house. Carpet on the floor muffled his footfalls. The walls were paneled in wood. He passed a painting of a mountain scene, another of a waterfall.

A maid in a black uniform and an apron came out of a room and gaped at him in astonishment. She was holding a feather duster and a cloth. "What in the world?"

"Where are they?" Fargo said.

"Where are who?"

"Joan Bascomb and Troy Utley. I saw them come in."

"I haven't seen Miss Bascomb in days, which is perfectly fine by me. And Troy Utley isn't to set foot in the door."

"Is the mayor here?"

"No, he's at his office, but two deputies are upstairs. The marshal has them watching the house after someone burned down—" She stopped and dropped the cloth and her hand rose to her throat. "Lord in heaven. You're him, aren't you? You're the lunatic who has been terrorizing the countryside."

"Are those your words or the mayor's?"

"His. But it must be true. Here you are with a gun in your hand."

"Why perfectly fine?" Fargo said.

The maid glanced toward a flight of stairs. "I'd rather not say."

"I was told she's a bitch."

"You were told rightly. If her father didn't pay so well, I wouldn't put up with her. She treats him like dirt, and me too, since I like him."

"Does she love Troy Utley?"

The maid flicked the feather duster across her chin. "The truth? I doubt that girl loves anyone but herself. Oh, she can put on a good front when she has to. I understand the Utleys think the world of her. But I know the real Joan. I know she tried to shoot her father in the back, not once but twice."

"The hell you say."

"I wouldn't lie. The first time was before they came here. The second time, I saved the mayor. He was in his study and she was sneaking up behind him with a derringer she got hold of. I yelled and she shot and missed and he took the derringer from her and called the doctor like he usually does when she has one of her fits."

"Fits?" Fargo said.

"That's what the mayor calls them. You ask me, that girl is plain mean-spirited."

"She told me he keeps her drugged so she can't run off with Troy."

"The mayor doesn't think the boy is right for her. But he also doesn't think she's right for the boy. She doesn't get her way, she turns violent."

"The mayor is no prize himself," Fargo said. "He rules this town with an iron fist."

"So?"

"You don't mind he does as he damn well pleases and runs roughshod over everyone?"

"We have a good town here, mister. He promised us it would always be peaceful and it was until you came along."

"Where are the deputies?"

The maid glanced at the stairs. "I'm not rightly sure. I've been cleaning and don't know where they got to."

"We're going up. Walk ahead of me. Don't scream. Don't yell to warn them."

"Or what? You'll shoot me?"

"I can be violent too," Fargo said.

She turned and moved in short steps to the foot of the stairs. "I'm asking you to reconsider. This will end with bloodshed if you don't."

"Up you go."

The maid obeyed but she moved like molasses. Near the top she stopped and whispered. "I'm begging you."

"I leave and Troy Utley might die."

"Is that all you care about? The Utley boy?"

"I promised his mother I'd get him home safe."

"What are the Utleys to you?"

"The deputies," Fargo said. "Now."

She dragged her feet to within a few feet of a closed door and pointed. "In there," she whispered. "It gives them a good view of the street."

Fargo opened the door and pushed her in ahead of him, and she gasped and froze. He was braced for shouts or shots but not two bodies in pools of spreading blood. One was in the middle of the room, the other by the window. He went to the nearest and dropped to a knee. "Stabbed in the back."

"It had to be Joan," the maid said.

The man at the window was sprawled facedown, scarlet oozing from a hole between his shoulder blades. Fargo saw that the deputy's holster was empty. So was the holster of the other one. "They were killed for their six-guns."

"She's after her father. We have to warn him."

"Where's his office?"

"Down the street a ways. I can take you if you want."

"Lead the way," Fargo said. He was puzzled when she abruptly stopped in the doorway and let out a grunt. Then she slowly turned, her face horror-struck, the hilt of a knife jutting from between her breasts.

22

The maid tried to speak and reached out to him. Instinctively, Fargo caught her as she fell, which was why his Colt was pointed at the floor when Joan Bascomb stepped into the room and gouged a cocked revolver against his temple.

"I'll take that," she said, and grabbed the Colt.

Fargo held on to it. "No."

"I'll shoot you if I have to. Don't think I won't."

Fargo was good at reading people. It was why he won so often at poker. The set of their face, their posture, sometimes the look in their eyes, told him whether they were bluffing or had the cards to back their bets. One look into Joan Bascomb's eyes and he knew she wasn't bluffing. He let go and she stepped back and beamed.

"Smart man. I like you but I won't let you or anyone else get in my way."

The maid had gone limp. Large red drops fell from her chest to the floor.

"Why in hell did you kill her?"

"She was fond of my father." Joan showed no regret or remorse. "I should have done it long ago."

"And the deputies?" Fargo said, with a bob of his head at their bodies.

"We needed their pistols."

"We?" Fargo said. As if he couldn't guess.

Troy Utley came to her side. He was holding a six-shooter.

"How are my folks?"

"Your pa was resting in bed the last I saw," Fargo said. "Your mother is worried sick."

"I won't let anything happen to him," Joan said.

"Looking after you, is she?" Fargo said.

Embarrassed, Troy replied, "I can look after myself. I don't need help from anyone."

"You will if you go through with your sweetheart's scheme," Fargo said.

"What do you know?" Joan said mockingly.

"That you want Troy to kill your father for you," Fargo said. "He's so in love with you, he's probably agreed."

"It's only right," Troy said.

"How do you figure?"

"It's not fitting for a daughter to kill her own pa. I'll gladly do it if we'll be free to live as we want."

"You mean after you get out of prison," Fargo said, "and provided they don't hang you."

"No one can prove it was me unless they see me do it and no one is going to see me do it except Joan," Troy said.

"And I'll say we were miles away at the time," Joan said sweetly. "I'm his alibi."

"Most of the town knows you hate your father," Fargo said.

"So? Hating him and killing him are two different things. Plus I'm a girl and girls don't go around murdering people."

"We have it all thought out," Troy boasted.

Fargo would have felt sorry for them if they weren't so dumb.

"Can I set the woman you just killed down now?"

"Oh. Sure." Joan wagged her revolver. "But no tricks, hear? You've been a big help to us and you're going to be a bigger help yet."

"I must have missed that part."

"We saw your horse out back," Joan said. "We're taking it with us and leaving it behind my father's office." She held his Colt up. "We're leaving this beside his body after Troy shoots him with it."

"You little bitch."

"Now, now. It's not enough for us to be our own alibi. As you pointed out, everyone knows my father and me don't get along." Joan smirked. "Just as everyone knows that you burned down our country house and have it in for him."

"I played right into your hands," Fargo said.

"Not really. I didn't have a plan beyond wanting him dead. But when I saw you ride up out back, I had an inspiration." Joan laughed. "Pretty clever of me, if I say so, myself."

"I think you're smart as sin," Troy told her.

"Now you'll tie me up, I suppose?" Fargo would die before he'd let them.

"Why in the world would we do that?" Joan responded. "You can't have shot my father if you're trussed up."

"I'll stop you."

"How? We have your pistol and your rifle is on your horse."

"Come anywhere near us and we'll shoot you," Troy threatened.

When Fargo didn't respond, Joan giggled. "Cat got your tongue? Nothing to say?"

"You sure ain't going to the law," Troy said. "Marshal Travers will shoot you the moment he sets eyes on you."

"Or maybe you think you can testify against us in court if they put you on trial," Joan brought up. "It will be your word against ours, and who do you think they'll believe after all you've done?"

"Damn," Fargo said.

"We have you over a barrel," Joan gloated. "We'll kill my father and incriminate you and live happily ever after."

"Ain't life grand?" Troy said.

Joan and Troy made Fargo sit on the bed in her father's bedroom and one or the other covered him while the other donned clothes from her father's closet. They both put on bowlers, Joan tucking her hair up into hers so that she appeared to be a man.

Fargo had to hand it to them. They didn't miss a trick. Or, rather, Joan didn't. Troy let her do all the thinking.

They warned him not to try anything, and left him there. From a back window he watched them lead the Ovaro off.

The moment they were out of sight Fargo was out the back door and to the fence. He levered his legs over and turned toward the main street. He didn't see a man come around the house next door but he heard the click of a gun hammer.

"Stop right there."

Fargo saw who it was, and swore.

"I couldn't believe my eyes when I saw you come out of the mayor's," Deputy Olsen said. "Marshal Travers will give me a bonus for this."

"I need your help," Fargo said.

Olsen came within a few steps. His hat was lopsided; he couldn't pull it down on one side because of a gash where Rosemary had bashed him with the rock. "*You* need *my* help?"

"Joan Bascomb is fixing to kill her father."

"Do you take me for a simpleton?"

"Go in the mayor's house and you'll find two dead deputies and a dead maid. She killed them."

Olsen glanced at the house. "Hank and Tom are dead?"

"Stabbed," Fargo said.

"By Joan?"

"You must know how much she hates him," Fargo said. "She's going to shoot him and leave my Colt and my horse to make everyone think I'm to blame."

"You never give up."

"Look at my holster. Do you think I'd come into town unarmed?"

Deputy Olsen glanced down. "Where's your six-gun?"

"I just told you."

"Peculiar," Olsen said. "I can't see you running around without it."

"Take me to the mayor's office before it's too late."

"Why should you want to warn him? You burned down his country house, for God's sake."

"Olsen, listen. I could have shot you the other day but I didn't."

"You wanted me to pass on a message."

Fargo talked faster. "I don't give a damn about the mayor. You're right about that. But I do give a damn about being blamed for something I didn't do. In a minute or two you'll hear some shots and it will be Joan doing what she has wanted to do for years."

"I almost believe you."

"Then how about this? You stay behind me and tell me which way to go and maybe we can get there in time to stop her."

"I don't know."

"You'll have me covered the whole time."

"Jesus," Olsen suddenly said, and paled.

"What?"

"I just remembered. The marshal is at the mayor's office. Him and that gal he's been courting, the schoolmarm."

"Susan Brubaker?" Fargo was on Olsen before the deputy could blink. He grabbed Olsen's wrist and twisted it so that the revolver pointed at the ground and not at him. Olsen cursed and tried to wrest loose but couldn't.

"Let go, damn you."

"Only if you get it through your head I'm not going to hurt you."

"I don't believe you," Olsen said, and swung.

Fargo had reached the limit of his patience. He slugged Olsen in his flabby gut and Olsen squealed and doubled over. A quick wrench, and Fargo had the revolver. Fear twisted Olsen's face and he thrust out an arm.

"Don't kill me! Please!"

Fargo spun the revolver so the grips were toward the deputy. "Will this convince you?"

"What the hell?"

"Take it. It's not a trick. We have to stop Joan and we're running out of time."

Olsen looked at the revolver and then at Fargo. "Son of a bitch."

"How far to the office?"

Olsen took the revolver and moved unsteadily toward the street. "It's around the corner and about three blocks down."

"We'll never make it."

They ran, Olsen waving his six-shooter and bawling at people to get out of their way. Most scattered like frightened chickens. Riders stopped to stare.

"Just one block to go," Olsen huffed. "See that sign yonder?"

Fargo had forgotten how much Bascomb liked signs. A large one proclaimed that it was the PROMISE MUNICIPAL BUILDING. He pulled ahead of Olsen.

The door to the Municipal Building opened and out stepped Marshal Lloyd Travers with Susan Brubaker's arm in his. They turned the other way.

Fargo didn't call out, not when Travers might go for his pistol.

Deputy Olsen didn't share Fargo's caution. "Marshal!" he hollered. "Marshal Travers!"

The lawman looked over his shoulder, saw Fargo, and did exactly as Fargo thought he would; Travers went into a crouch, his hand stabbing for his revolver.

"No!" Olsen bawled.

Travers didn't hear him or didn't care. The revolver cleared the holster.

Fargo saw the muzzle rise, and dived flat. The boom of the lawman's revolver was echoed by another in the municipal building.

"Don't shoot! Don't shoot!" Deputy Olsen screamed.

Fargo rolled toward a parked buckboard and scrambled under it as Travers fired again. The slug kicked up dirt inches from his face. He made it out the other side as the horse, spooked, bolted, and the buckboard clattered off.

Marshal Travers was taking deliberate aim.

Fargo was in the middle of the street with nowhere to hide. He tensed to throw himself to one side, and suddenly Olsen was between them, flapping his arms and yelling for Travers to lower his pistol.

It was then that Susan Brubaker screamed.

The mayor came stumbling out of his office. His hands were over his belly and his fingers were slick with bright blood. He had the strangest expression. He raised an imploring hand to the schoolmarm and fell to his knees.

"Help me!"

Out of the office came Joan Bascomb, her face a mask of

pure hate. She had Fargo's Colt. From a distance of no more than three feet she pointed it at the back of her father's head and squeezed the trigger. Hair and bits of skull and pieces of brain flew in all directions. Blood spurted out of her father's mouth, and he pitched forward.

Travers and Olsen were rooted in disbelief. Olsen jerked his pistol first and fired but in his haste he missed. The shot seemed to bring Joan out of herself. She snapped her head up, saw them, and shot Marshal Travers in the face. Behind her, in the doorway, Troy appeared. Holding his revolver in both hands, he fired at Olsen.

Fargo was in motion. He needed a revolver and the nearest was on the ground next to Travers. A slug buzzed his ear. Another clipped his shirt. He dived again and caught hold of the six-gun and was up on a knee.

Deputy Olsen had a hole in his throat. Gurgling and wheezing and spraying blood, he clutched at his neck.

Troy Utley put another slug into him.

Joan was retreating into the office.

Fargo aimed at her but Troy shifted and fired at him and his hat went flying. Fargo didn't hesitate. He had promised Rosemary but it was the boy or him. He shot Troy in the chest. Troy was punched onto his toes but gamely fired and missed. Fargo shot him a second time. Troy lurched half around and in reflex worked the hammer and the trigger and got off a final shot. But the revolver wasn't pointing at Fargo. It was pointed at the schoolmarm.

Susan Brubaker shrieked. High on the left side of her yellow dress a red stain blossomed. She teetered and looked down at herself and then in terrified appeal at Fargo. He saw the life fade from her eyes and the blank emptiness that replaced it.

Troy was on the ground, convulsing.

Fargo leaped over him and against the wall. Inside the office his own Colt banged. Lead sent slivers from the jamb. He risked a peek but didn't see her. There were desks and chairs and a cabinet to the right. From the sound of the shot he suspected she was behind the cabinet. He launched himself through the doorway and landed on his side.

Joan Bascomb rose from behind a desk only a few feet away. She had him dead to rights. The Colt was cocked and steady.

She grinned over the barrel. "He was harder to kill than I thought. But you won't be." She squeezed the trigger.

They both heard the click.

"No," Joan said.

Fargo pointed the revolver at the point where her nose met her forehead.

"You wouldn't."

The office rocked to a final blast.

Rosemary had a Bible in her hands and her head bowed. Clyde's arm was in a sling. Only a few townspeople had come to the funeral. The minister finished with the eulogy and offered his condolences and left.

"Where will you go?" Rosemary asked.

"Wherever the wind takes me," Fargo said. He put a hand on her arm. "It couldn't be helped."

"I know. A lot of folks saw it. They all say he shot at you, that you had no choice." Rosemary's eyes watered and she groaned. "God, I loved him."

"It was her," Fargo said.

"Yes." Rosemary nodded. "She had a sickness in her. Poor Troy couldn't see it."

Fargo put his hat on and adjusted his bandanna. He stared at the fresh pile of earth and the flowers that lay on top of it and at the headstone that read, HERE LIES TROY UTLEY, KILLED BY BAD LOVE. "Whose idea was that?"

"Mine," Rosemary said.

Fargo nodded at each of them and walked from the cemetery. Unwrapping the reins, he climbed on the Ovaro. "Let's get the hell out of here."

He didn't look back.

LOOKING FORWARD!
The following is the opening
section of the next novel in the exciting
***Trailsman* series from Signet:**

TRAILSMAN #352
TEXAS TANGLE

The badlands of Texas, 1861—where death
is always a heartbeat away.

There were so many buzzards that from far off they looked like a swarm of flies.

Skye Fargo was crossing the baked plains of central Texas when he spied the dark devourers of the dead in the pale blue sky. He could ignore them and ride on to Fort Lancaster. Instead, he reined the Ovaro toward them. He didn't know what he would find. It might be the remains of slaughtered buffalo. That many buzzards, there had to be a lot of dead.

Fargo was a tall man, broad of shoulder and narrow at the hip. He always wore buckskins, and was partial to a white hat and red bandanna. The buckskins were a clue to his stock-in-trade; he was a scout, and a good one. He knew the ways of the wild lands better than most any man alive, which was why he now put his hand on his Colt.

There had to be fifty of the big birds, their black wings outspread, their grotesque featherless heads as red as the blood of the kills they dined on.

Fargo climbed a low rise and drew rein. "Damn," he said to the empty air.

Five Conestogas were strung along the bank of a creek. They weren't moving. They couldn't; their teams had been taken. The canvas tops hung in strips. The belongings of those who owned the wagons were scattered all over, and scattered among the belongings were their bodies.

Fargo scanned the prairie. Other than the vultures nothing moved. He gigged the Ovaro.

A particularly large buzzard was pecking at the eye socket of a dead woman. It plucked the eyeball out and gulped it with a flick of its long neck, then bent to the other eye.

Fargo shot it. At the blast, the buzzards feasting on other figures hissed and flapped to get airborne. One buzzard flew right at him and he raised the Colt but the bird banked and soared over his head.

Fargo came to a burly man in overalls whose throat had been ravaged by the beaks of the hungry birds. The man's eyes hadn't been touched. They were wide open and glazed and mirrored sheer horror.

Fargo climbed down. He held on to the reins as he went from body to body. Not that he had any doubts. A broken arrow told him who was to blame. They were thorough, the Comanches. He stepped over a grandfather clock, its mechanical innards strewn about. He moved amid pots and pans and clothes and tools. No weapons, though. The Comanches wouldn't leave those.

Fargo came to the body of a woman who had been cut from belly to neck. Her intestines had spilled out and one of her ears was missing.

A groan caused Fargo to stiffen. He went around a covered wagon. Near it lay a middle-aged man, twitching. The man had no clothes. Nor fingers or toes. His nose was missing. Incredibly, he was still alive. As Fargo came over, he blinked and licked his parched lips.

"Thank God."

Fargo squatted in a pool of dry blood. "I can get you to the fort if you want."

The man said something in a hoarse whisper.

"I didn't catch that," Fargo said, and bent his ear to the man's lips.

"Kill me."

Fargo straightened.

"Put me out of my misery. Please."

"There's a chance," Fargo said.

"No, there's not," the man replied. "I'm a goner and we both know it."

Fargo didn't say anything.

The man let out a sob. "They hit us out of nowhere just as it got dark. Twenty or more. We didn't even see them but we heard them whoop and holler. There wasn't time to circle the wagons."

"It wouldn't have helped," Fargo said. Not against that many.

"Half the men were down before the rest could lift a gun.

I was in our wagon looking for the axle grease and my wife was driving or I'd have been killed outright too."

"The Comanches have been on a rampage lately," Fargo said. "No one knows why."

"Hell, mister, they don't need an excuse." The man coughed and blood trickled from a corner of his mouth.

"Would you like some water?"

"God, would I."

Fargo fetched his canteen. He opened it and carefully tilted it. The man gulped and sighed.

"I'm obliged."

"How many were in your party?" Fargo asked. He'd counted twelve bodies.

"Seventeen, counting me."

"Hell," Fargo said.

"They took four women. The youngest. Why them and not anyone else I couldn't say. I heard them screaming as they were dragged off."

"Maybe the warriors took a shine to them." Fargo was being optimistic. A lot of tribes, the Apaches, for instance, thought white women were too puny to make good wives.

"You have to go after them. You have to save them."

"Twenty Comanches and one of me." Fargo didn't mind the high odds but twenty Comanches were twenty Comanches.

"Go to Fort Lancaster, then. Tell the colonel what happened. Tell him one of the women they took was his daughter, Miranda."

"Maybe you shouldn't talk. You might last longer."

"Who wants to last?" The man weakly grasped Fargo's sleeve. "I asked you before. I'm asking you again. Kill me."

Fargo had put horses out of their misery. And once a mule.

It was never a task he liked.

The man let out a ragged gasp. "Tell me you'll get word to the army."

"I'll get word."

The beating of heavy wings drew Fargo's gaze to the sky. More vultures were arriving. When he looked down, the man's eyes were empty of life. He felt for a pulse but there wasn't any.

Fargo checked the rest of the bodies. He noticed that every single one had been shot. Not one had been knifed or pierced by an arrow or transfixed by a lance. Yet there had been that broken arrow. When he was satisfied they were all dead he climbed on the Ovaro and roved in circles until he found where the attackers had gone off to the northwest. He figured they had a good day and a half start on him, maybe more. As much as he wanted to help the women, he had to be realistic. Reluctantly, he reined around and tapped his spurs.

Behind him, the dark legion descended.

No other series packs this much heat!

THE TRAILSMAN

Follow the trail of Penguin's Action Westerns at
penguin.com/actionwesterns

S310